STEALING TIME

Nicky Edwards

Published by Onlywomen Press, Ltd.
Radical Feminist and Lesbian publishers,
38 Mount Pleasant, London WC1X 0AP.

Printed and bound in Denmark by Nørhaven.
Typeset by Columns, Reading, Berks, UK.

British Library Cataloguing in Publication Data
Edwards, Nicky
Stealing Time.
I. Title
823'.914 [F]

ISBN 0–906500–31–1

****

Thanks to Penny Florence, Jen Green, Jinno Lillington and Sasha Roseneil.

London at the turn of the century was a city of contrasts. An army of beggars patrolled the streets along which the rich, in evening dress, passed on their way to the opera. Filthy smogs gripped the chests of rich and poor alike, but were less easily shut out of the houses, thrown up when the Queen and the century were both middle-aged, to accommodate the working classes. Many of these buildings were crumbling, as their inhabitants succumbed to diseases of poverty, old age and neglect. Health was as much a topic in the West End, as in the East, with those peddling food fads and patent medicines doing a brisk trade as a result of sensational advertisements. Public sanitation was a growing scandal and concern; sweatshops throve and children were prostituted.

Thus it was in London, in 1999. . .

* * *

Al's classroom was a cabin, formerly building-site office, donated by one of the PTA when his construction firm had no more use for it. The desks had been made, not very sturdily, by young offenders in a community service unit. The pupils brought their own chairs. The school couldn't afford chairs. It could barely pay its (short) complement of teachers. Three or four were always sacked towards the end of the financial year, to ease the payroll problem.

She waited until the security men had plodded past on their round, alsatian in tow. They attempted to stop the pupils from wrecking the school, or each other, or themselves. There were a thousand other children on the roll, apart from Al, and few of them more law-abiding, even than herself.

Al slipped out from her classroom. It was tucked away, out of sight and mind, past the old boiler room, behind the boys' toilets. The smarter mobile classrooms were stacked three high in what used to be the playground. She walked quickly into the main school block, hoping she looked small enough not to attract the attention of security men, but not so small that she got mugged. The effect was adolescent, spiky-haired tough.

The computing workshops were on the third floor. Her class were never allowed to use them, but she knew where to go. She whistled casually, and got some strange looks from the other people on the staircase. Not being able to hear the noise she made, Al had never learned to whistle properly, but she associated whistling, the puckered lips and hands in pockets, with harmlessness and a clear conscience.

In the workshop, the computing club was waiting for the teacher-in-charge to arrive. Al fell immediately for the long, tidy room, its rows of screens and keyboards. She sat herself down at a terminal in the corner. A few of the others stared at her, a strange face, but no-one spoke.

The teacher arrived, late and flustered. He glanced around the room and saw Al, amusing herself by debugging the "learner" programme.

"That girl in the corner," he shouted. "Stop it. Come over here. Don't touch anything." Al had her back to him, and didn't realise she was being addressed. The girl at the next workstation nudged her in the ribs and jerked her head in the direction of the teacher.

"You deaf or something?" she asked. Al smiled non-committally. The teacher marched over and seized Al by the shoulder.

"Don't touch anything. These aren't toys." He shook her. The girl became aware of his presence and stood up, facing him.

"I want to join the computer club."

"Never use a terminal without permission," he fussed. "I don't know why one of the others didn't tell you," he glared round him. "What's your name, anyway?"

"Alison Treece."

"It's twenty Europounds termly enrolment, plus five per session. You know that?"

Al watched his lips moving as he spoke, and nodded, "Yes, I've got the credit."

"Let's have your school ID," he grumbled. "You should have joined three weeks ago, like the others."

She handed over a plastic card with a series of bar codes on it. The teacher fed it into a machine which read the black lines and clicked quietly to itself.

"You're a remedial." The teacher looked shocked. Al stuck her hands in her pockets and set her jaw.

"So?" she looked up at him obstinately.

"We can't have you in here," he fretted. "My god, a dozen car-boot sales to buy one wretched unit. There's no way I'm going to have some half-wit from remedial blundering about here. Go away." He flapped his hands crossly.

"I was doing alright." Al stayed, stubbornly, pointing at the screen on which she had saved her work. The teacher glanced at it and turned pale.

"Who called that programme up for you? Has no-one here any sense of responsibility?" He sat down at the terminal and started hurriedly checking the programme. Al watched him, angry and contemptuous.

"Go away, you stupid girl," he turned to look at her with loathing. "Get back to your counting games and cardboard collages." He tapped worriedly at the cursor shift. "Go on, if you're not out of here in ten seconds, I'll call security."

Al turned and left. "Really," the teacher muttered, "the things I have to put up with."

* * *

Al dawdled her way back to her classroom. "Where's Marcie?" she asked the girls sitting on the heater, dodging the splashes of condensation which dropped from the window frame.

"Round the back," said one. "With Karen."

"Karen's in a state," added her friend. "She's got one up the gut."

"Silly cow thought she couldn't get pregnant if she did it standing up," said a third girl. "Still, there's no point crying over spilt milk." They all laughed.

At that moment, Karen walked in, her face puffy and blotched with tears. There was a second of silence, as everyone stopped what they were doing and stared at her knowingly.

"Ooh, Karen, what you gonna call it?" asked the leader of the trio on the heater.

"Can we use the baby in Parentcraft, when you have it?" asked another of the gang. "Better than bathing a doll."

"At least you didn't take it lying down," shouted one of the boys from the far end of the room. Karen turned and fled, pursued by screams of laughter. Al left her classmates to enjoy the joke and climbed down the rickety steps which led from the door of the portakabin to the ground.

Between the mobile classroom and the school wall behind it, was a narrow alley, hidden from prying eyes and seldom visited by security patrols. Marcie leaned against the mossy green brickwork of the wall, drinking from a bottle of pineapple juice. She offered the bottle to Al.

"What's it got in it?" Al took a cautious mouthful.

"Light rum. It'll warm you up."

"Where'd you get it?"

"Robbed it off my dad. He won't notice, the old soak."

Al handed the bottle back, politely wiping the neck clean with her hand.

"What was all the row in there?" asked Marcie, having knocked back another slug of rum.

"The three wise monkeys having a go at Karen. Well, everybody was, but you know what they're like."

"If they weren't such a bunch of slags, it'd make you wonder, wouldn't it, the way you never see one of them without the other two. Lesbe friends." Marcie nudged Al in the ribs. "Still, I don't know why they're giving Karen a hard time. Could've been one of them, just as easy."

"Karen ran off somewhere. She won't stand up to them."

"Her lift don't go all the way to the top floor," sighed Marcie. "I had her crying on my shoulder. I give her a drink, but I think that was her trouble in the first place. And he must've been pretty out of it at the time. She's not exactly a picture, is she?"

The hooter sounded for the end of break. Marcie retrieved the bottle from Al and turned to go. Al, deducing the noise from the action, followed, stepping carefully past the other two occupants of the alley, a girl from her class and an older boy who were locked in a lip-chapping embrace. The boy was exploring inside his partner's clothes, his arm contorted through several layers, with the minute attention of one who has dropped a contact lens. One of the girl's breasts, prised out of its bra, was visible in the resulting dishevelment. Al noticed the blue-tinged, goose-pimple fringed nipple, and shivered.

"They'll freeze off if you leave them hanging out in this weather," she said, daringly, before hurrying off out of reach of any answer.

Mrs Callum, the teacher responsible for events and sponsorship, was waiting for them in the school hall. "Numbers on the left, pom-poms on the right," she shouted. Three hundred pupils milled around, enjoying the confusion. "Three R," she called to Al's class, "where are your pom-poms?"

"Ain't got none," they chorused.

"Well, tell your parents you must have them before the next rehearsal," she ordered, distractedly. "In the meantime, you must pretend." 3R and the other classes were marshalled into position. Al noticed a tearful Karen slip into the back row, and take her place.

"Music, please," called Mrs Callum, and the fourth movement of Beethoven's ninth blared out across the hall. Al stood in a semi-circle with the rest of her year, waving imaginary pom-poms over her head, irritated by the muffled irregular booming, which was all she heard of the Ode to Joy. Into the space partly enclosed by the pom-pom wavers shuffled the rest of the performers, pushed and shepherded by distracted teachers. They organised themselves roughly into the shape of a two and a one. The semi-circle of third years closed in on them menacingly.

"No," shouted Mrs Callum, leaping down from the stage into the middle of the throng. "We're supposed to be rehearsing for the opening ceremony of the Festival of Europe, not Custer's Last Stand. You pom-poms, don't crowd in like that. Stand back, make a proper C. You're welcoming the 21st century, not strangling it at birth." A hundred and fifty pairs of feet shuffled reluctantly backwards. "Just think what it'll be like on the day – there'll be thousands of you in the stadium, and everyone of you has to be in the right place at the right time. What's it going to look like on television, if you can't even manage to make a simple little C21? It's not as if you were being asked to do the Polish flag."

The rehearsal started again. Al tried to imagine what they would look like from above, equipped with their coloured pom-poms. They had four months in which to practice, before the festival opened in the summer, but she thought it would probably be a mess. Mrs Callum, back up on the stage, was wearing a teeshirt which said 'Festival of Europe, 1999' on the front, and 'Unity, Security & Enterprise' on the back. Al wondered whether any freebies would be coming the way of the performers, but thought it unlikely.

Her interest in the proceedings, which had been slight to start with, waned altogether. Her arms were beginning to ache, and she stopped bothering to wave them at the same tempo as those about her, who were, anyway, behaving more like a football crowd than a cultural event. Marcie, standing beside her, was squirming with discomfort, her bladder full of alcohol. She smelt rummy, like a christmas pudding.

Suddenly a teacher appeared in front of Al, whose non-conformist waving was disrupting the look of the front row.

"In time to the music," he instructed, waving his hands over his head to demonstrate. "Concentrate. Listen to the music."

"She can't hear it," said Marcie, helpfully. Al glowered at the young teacher.

"Why not? She's got a pair of ears, hasn't she?"

"They don't work."

"Oh," the teacher was nonplussed, but soon recovered himself. "Beethoven was deaf, you know. And he wrote this."

"Beethoven didn't have to wave a pair of poxy pom-poms over his head while he was doing it," snapped Al.

"I thought you said she was deaf," protested the teacher to Marcie.

"Hearing impaired," said Al, who disliked being talked about.

"Alright, you two, out." He lost patience. "If you're not going to take this seriously. You can tell your parents you've been dropped from the display."

"They'll be gutted," said Al, before Marcie grabbed her by the arm and dragged her out of the hall.

"I'm bustin'," Marcie declared, heading for the toilets.

"It's my day for getting thrown out," complained Al, peering at herself in the mirror. "First the computer workshop, then the rehearsal. . ."

"Waste of time, both of them," Marcie emerged from the cubicle to wash her hands. Finding that she couldn't lip read in the mirror, Al turned to face her friend. "Anyway, you only got thrown out of a class. Not like Karen's going to get. At least you ain't pregnant."

"Don't you ever worry about it?"

"Who says I've done anything to worry about?"

"You did."

"I never," Marcie protested.

"Well, you drop enough hints. Everyone thinks you have."

"Dirty minds you've all got."

"If you did, wouldn't it worry you? What you might catch, even if you didn't end up like Karen?"

"*If* I did," said Marcie, with chilly emphasis, "I'd be careful."

"Bet that's what Karen said."

"She's thick, that's her trouble. Didn't take precautions."

"I don't know why you bother."

"Because otherwise they say you're frigid." Marcie examined a spot. "Anyway, it's normal, it's what everyone does."

"It's what everyone talks about. Anyway, I don't."

"That's different."

"Why?"

"Boys are funny about. . ."

"Spastic mutant retard cloth-eared cripples?" suggested Al.

"Yeah, well," Marcie was embarrassed. "You could let your hair grow a bit."

"Why?" Al looked in the mirror again. "It's fashionable."

"It's not very," Marcie looked for the word, "flattering. And you don't shave your legs. Or your armpits."

"How do you know?" Al was surprised. "About my armpits?"

"I seen them in the changing room. Other girls notice too."

"It's a good thing I don't know when you're all whispering behind my back," said Al, bitterly.

"I didn't," Marcie defended herself.

"Actually, I do know. Bunch of bitches."

"It's unhygienic," sniffed Marcie. "Face it, Al, you're nearly fourteen. It's time you started acting your age. All you care about is computers and machines."

"You never complain when I get you free games in the arcade."

"That's just kids' stuff. I mean, you act like you're some kind of genius, but you're still in remedial with the rest of us. So what if you can fix things, you fail all your school assessments, same as me."

"Who cares?" Al shrugged. "School's boring."

"God, no wonder everyone treats you like their kid brother," Marcie was exasperated. "If you did get asked out. . ."

"Which I won't."

". . . you'd probably spend your first date tuning his car up, or something. You don't act like a girl should."

"So if I grew my hair, except for where I should shave it off, and acted as stupid as I'm supposed to be, you reckon I might get a boyfriend?"

"Yeah, maybe."

"Like Karen did? Or that poor tart who was freezing her tits off behind the class, while the boyfriend blasted her with slobber? It was like watching a church being restored. No thanks."

"Suit yourself," said Marcie pettishly. "But don't blame me if people think you're weird."

"I'm off home. You coming?"

"How'll you get out? The guards'll never let you through the door."

"Through the old block. There's a door onto Leeson Street."

"It's locked," protested Marcie.

"I'll unlock it."

"How?"

"With a stick of ozone friendly underarm deodorant," snappped Al. "You coming, or what?"

"The register," said Marcie. "If we're not here to check-out at leaving time, it'll flash our names to the attendance office."

"I can take care of it," Al shrugged.

"Don't be soft. It's a machine."

"You're soft, Marcie. There's nothing to hang round here for."

"It's better than being in class."

"It's colder. I'm going."

"You'll get caught," cautioned Marcie.

"And you'll die of boredom," replied Al, tartly. "See you tomorrow."

"Not if I see you first, spas," said Marcie quietly. Al, who had already turned her back, did not hear.

"I'm taking a mental health day," announced the receptionist. "You'll have to cover."

"Jean, how can you do this to me?" groaned Kerry, the junior technician. "Why don't you wait until you're really stressed and take a proper sickie?"

"It's zoo time out there," Jean indicated the swarms of waiting patients crowding the department of audiometry. "It's always like this in March. I hate the end of winter."

"Spring is in the air," Kerry encouraged. "Look out the window and see snow drops."

"From the sky, perhaps," snorted the other woman. "Not growing in the car park." A gust of sleet rattled against the window of the office in which they sat. Kerry perched on the heating unit in a gloom.

"I'm sure you're right," she conceded. "The only thing that ever drops around here are building slabs onto a pedestrian's head. And that's probably a plot by the organ-transplant team to recruit donors."

It was true that St. Jude's, Fulham, was not beautiful, even as hospitals go. The main block (circa 1978) had been faced with sludge-coloured vitreous panels. Two decades later, they were now detaching themselves at random, causing an upturn in the profitability of Accident and Emergency. Only the executive stress annexe was free of major structural defects.

Kerry was younger than her workplace, and in a better state of repair, with the help of a regular exercise class and badminton with the nurses. Being short, and rosy-cheeked, she did not look her nineteen years. This infuriated Kerry, although when mistaken for a half-fare on the bus, she never volunteered to pay the extra. Her bottle-blond hair was carefully arranged, not too short, not too femmy.

From school, via Work Experience and vocational training, Kerry had progressed to this, her maiden job. Desperate to escape from Guildford, she had taken the first post that was available in London. For two months after arriving, she had shared a single bed on a shift basis with a nurse who worked nights. As one of them finished work, the other would be getting up. At least the sheets had always been warm.

The receptionist having grumbled her way to the signing-out desk, Kerry braced herself to face the clamorous throng of the paying public. The other technicians were crowded round the reception area, complaining as they tried to call up patient records and check MediCred status. None of them enjoyed the bureaucracy which seemed to be half the working life of the hospital.

A man with two children in tow approached the desk, elbowing aside some less determined patients. Kerry took his MediCred card and punched up the index number.

"You've exhausted your allocation," she informed him. "Have you got a Supplementary Entitlement?"

The man growled and shook his head. One of his children, alerted by his clenched fists and rising colour, covered its face and cowered. Kerry could tell she was about to get bashed and felt for the panic button under the desk.

"Additional Personal Health Insurance?" she asked hopefully. "A top-up policy?" The man growled again. "Then you'll have to pay in advance or come back next month." She tried to sound calm. The outraged parent told her, quite graphically, what she could do with her payments in advance, and began kicking the reception desk. Other patients edged away, and Kerry looked wildly around for the security people. Two gangling youths in badly fitting uniforms appeared, took one look at the frustrated customer and radioed for reinforcements. Four of them eventually threw him out, helped by impatient people behind him in the queue. Kerry, rapidly filling out a report for the staff rep., wanted to sit down, but the incident was too routine to warrant personal time.

One of the nurses, who had witnessed the affair from a safe distance, brought Kerry a cup of tea, laced with something warming. Choking on the alcohol, she got a friendly pat on the back.

"You'll get used to it, dear," the nurse said cheerfully, "when you've been here as long as I have. Just be grateful you're not on Surgical. Pure murder."

Kerry thanked him for the drink. "St. Jude, you know," murmured the nurse, collecting the empty cup. "Patron saint of lost causes. Good, isn't it?"

The nurse bustled off and Kerry got back to business. She knew when she was well off, without having to be told. Although her workplace was shabby, she was reassured each day by the prominent 'NO HIV+ ADMITTED' notices posted at every entrance. Also the mandatory blood tests for all registered patients and staff. Watching one of the Nurse Helpers carelessly handling a cardboard disposal box full of used sharps, Kerry felt glad that only the basically healthy were allowed in her department. Dreadful stories had been told at her training college of hospitals too poor to choose whom they treated, administrators so desperate for MediCred, they would have no discrimination in their admissions policy at all.

A woman from somewhere near Cape Wrath presented her Area Health Authority Transfer Treatment voucher at the desk. There were no hospitals in her part of Scotland, it being more efficient to let the patients shop around the centres of excellence. Or get sent to where their treatment could be done at the cheapest rate, on the bulk-buying, economies-of-scale basis.

The woman, who had travelled for two days to keep her appointment, was profoundly deaf. Kerry had some trouble understanding her, but using her rudimentary sign language, she managed to complete the admissions procedure. Personally, she thought the consultant cheeky to consider operating in such a case, with little chance of success. She supposed he knew what he was doing. It was lucky the department did not get paid by results. When Kerry was more experienced, she would apply for a job at one of the higher grade hospitals, where customers with Medi-Cred Plus Gold Privilege cards were the norm, and you never had to cover an unfilled vacancy.

* * *

A woman trudged up the Old Kent Road. She had come from Rochester, pushing her belongings in a dilapidated pram. The pram caught its wheels frequently on the broken paving stones, and snagged on the sodden cardboard crates and plastic bags which littered the streets.

Beside her, a continuous line of juggernauts edged its way into London from the Channel Tunnel. The crunching gears and percussive hiss of brakes drowned out what the woman was saying, for she talked to herself as she stumped along.

Her hair was grey, like sleet on the spoil heap of a coal mine. She wore many layers of clothes, although the day was warm. Her face was tanned and dried from days on the road, and her bones grated rheumatically together from nights on the pavement.

She turned into an alley beside the A2(M). The alley stank of cat piss, the crumbling brickwork of its walls cut out most of the sulphurous yellow afternoon sunlight. Other itinerants came here, but today she was on her own.

The woman parked her pram and walked shakily to the large steel bin where the rubbish from the Chinese takeaway's kitchen was dumped. Most commercial garbage cans had locks, this one was old-fashioned. She rootled contentedly among the vegetable peelings and came out with a stripped down chicken carcass, and some bones to chew. It had been two days since her last meal. Carefully, she tucked a handful of carrot tops into the pram, against another hungry day, then she cleared a small space for herself on the concrete. Her feet hurt, her head spun, she needed a rest. Dizzily, she slid to the ground and passed out, or fell asleep, almost at once.

The policeman was large, young and fleshy. His boots crunched on the rubble in the alley. He shook the old woman roughly by the shoulder and spoke in a loud voice.

"Wakey wakey, rise and shine."

She mumbled something and opened her eyes. Behind the large policeman, the nervous proprietor of the Chinese takeaway hovered, casting her apologetic and harried glances.

"Got your ID?" the officer demanded, pulling her to her feet. "Pissed are you?"

She tried to speak, but her tongue felt sluggish. It had been days since she spoke to anyone apart from herself, sometimes she forgot how to make conversation. The policeman propped her against the wall and picked distastefully through the things in the pram.

"What's this?" He found the vegetable scraps and a chicken bone. "You pinch these from the bin here?"

"It's alright, officer," the man behind him began. "They're only rubbish."

"Shut up Chan. You know the law."

"Pay him for them." She suddenly found her voice, unsteady but loud enough.

"Oh, so it talks does it?" The policeman dropped the food and wiped his hands on a paper tissue.

"I'll pay him for them," she repeated, fiercely, rummaging in one of her pockets for an old leather purse. She took out a couple of brassy looking coins and gave them to the reluctant shop owner.

"What the bloody hell's that?" The policeman peered at the coins. "If he wanted washers, he'd go down the hardware."

"Money," she said stubbornly.

"Not any more it isn't, granny. That's a handful of scrap." He turned to the man beside him and tapped his forehead significantly. "Better get you somewhere you can't hurt yourself."

"Not hurting anyone," she sagged against the wall, exhausted. A cloud of grit and lorry fumes blew up the alley, making her cough.

"Come on then, where's your ID?" The policeman finished radioing for a secure ambulance.

"Haven't got one." Her eyes were shut, she seemed absent from the proceedings.

"Don't be a silly old bag, of course you've got one. We can't put you in the nice hospital if you won't give us your Social Credit number, can we?"

"Haven't got one," she said again. The policeman began searching her many pockets and bags, but found no plastic identity.

"What have you done with it? Lost it, have you?" He spoke loudly and slowly, so as to make her understand.

"Never had one," she mumbled. "I'm a traveller."

"Bloody old tramp," the constable muttered. He got on the radio and cancelled the ambulance, called for a police van instead. The takeaway owner crept quietly back down the alley and vanished.

"I'll have to arrest you then, you old nuisance. Failing to produce required documents. Trespass, vagrancy and theft." He took her by the arm and led her towards the road.

"My things." She clutched at the pram.

"Leave that rubbish here." He tugged at her sleeve. "You'll stink up the station bad enough as it is."

"My things," she said again, more quietly. Then she set her face determinedly blank and allowed herself to be led off to wait for the police van.

Dawn broke reluctantly along Duncannon Street and into Trafalgar Square, daylight easily outdone by streetlight, as Donna Treece trudged up from Whitehall to catch her bus home.

She walked without looking ahead of her, the route familiar after years. There was an unkind wind blowing rain down the neck of the too-thin man's overcoat in which she huddled. One hand was tucked deep in the patch pocket, the other, holding a carrier bag, looked chapped and sore, used to being left out in the cold. Teams of dispirited youths in the uniforms of a clean-up charity earned their benefits by fishing rubbish out of the fountains at the base of Nelson's column. At the bus stop a few people stood waiting hopefully beside the unlit, shut-up bus that would be theirs when the driver appeared. One of the women in the queue looked up as Donna approached and smiled at her from over the scarf wrapped around her neck and lower jaw.

"Morning, Donna."

"Daff," she nodded her acknowledgement, putting down her bag on the pavement.

"Good weekend?"

"It was OK. I didn't do anything special."

"Sleep's pretty special to me."

Donna laughed, croakily. "Sleep? What's that?"

"You working overtime?"

"Double-shift," she stamped her feet in their woolly-lined boots on the pavement, but her circulation had a whole night of standing up to avenge.

"Rather you than me. Even for time and a quarter." She yawned.

"I need some extra at the moment. And the rent's due," Donna explained.

"I'm always behind," Daff agreed. She took out a pack of cigarettes and offered one.

"I shouldn't, I'm trying to give up."

"Go on. Give yourself a treat."

"Oh, well. Thanks." Donna lit up gratefully. "We're not allowed to smoke at work. It's a sackable offence."

"You never!"

"True. They put it in their bid when they went for the contract."

"I'd not stand for that. Got to have a fag-break."

"We didn't have a lot of choice. Plenty of others would be glad of the chance, as they like to keep reminding us. Anyway, they're right, it is a filthy habit."

"S'pose so," Daff coughed. "How's your kid?"

"Alison's alright. I've got to take her to the hospital today. More tests."

"What's she got, then?"

"Secretory otitis media."

Daff looked blank. "Come again?"

"Glue ear."

"She deaf?"

"No. It's difficult for her, that's all. Hearing impaired. She can't hear you talking if you're more than half a metre away."

"Well then." Daff picked up her bag as the bus driver appeared, opened the door, hopped on and shut it behind him as he settled himself in the driving seat. Eventually he opened the doors again and the damp queue filed on. Donna and Daff punched their travel strips along with the others and found a seat together.

"They doing anything for her? The hospital?"

"There's an operation for it." Donna squeezed further along the seat as the bus filled and a crowd stood in the aisles. "She's on the waiting list."

"Bloody hell, how'd you manage that?"

"I had to buy an extra health package for the operation. That's one of the reasons I've been working late. But she's entitled – she's got enough Social Credit."

"Don't get me wrong, Donna, if I say I wouldn't have thought your rating was high enough. Though god knows that kid of yours is a nice little girl."

"No offence taken. Her Social Credit rating was 2.2. Not enough to get you into an evening class at the tech."

"So how'd you fix it then? Go on, I won't tell, if it's a bit, you know. . ." she winked.

"No, there's nothing to tell," Donna was vague. "Somebody else had more credits than they needed and transferred a few to Alison."

"Didn't know you could do that."

"Oh yes."

"Must've been a pretty good friend."

"Not really. It's someone from the church I belong to."

"Charity, eh?"

"We try and help one another out," Donna agreed.

"Oh." Daff didn't look entirely convinced, but didn't press it. "Good luck to you, is all I can say."

They chatted on about kids and hospitals until the bus lumbered up to the clump of tower blocks dumped in a marsh, where Donna lived. The lift was full of rubbish and graffiti, but at least it worked, on and off. Today was on. She took it to the ninth floor, unfastened the three locks on her front door and stepped into the flat. She could hear Alison clattering about in the kitchen. Donna hung up her coat and kissed her daughter good morning.

"Hi, Mum." The girl wiped crumbs and jam from her mouth to return the kiss. She was short, but compactly built, not skinny. Her voice was pitched only slightly too loud.

"Want some toast?"

"Please." She took off her boots and rubbed her feet into slippers.

Al went back to the grill, knowing better than to chat to Donna first thing. It was a shame Donna was so grumpy when she got in from working a double-shift, Al was full of energy in the mornings and wanted to talk about what was lined up for the day ahead. She sat down quietly opposite Donna with her pointed chin resting on the heels of her hands, elbows on the table. She had a broad, square forehead, with strong eyebrows.

Grateful for the silence, Donna finished her breakfast and stood up. "Get your things, Alison, we're going to the hospital."

"Why have I got to go again?"

"Don't ask me."

"I don't want to go. I don't like the hospital."

"That makes two of us."

"Let's not go." Al looked hopeful.

"No, we must. How are you ever going to get better if we don't go to see the doctor?"

"We've seen him lots already and I still got gluey ears."

"You'll be better when you've had the operation. Maybe." Donna was getting them both into outdoor clothes while they went through this ritual.

"Maybe?" Al was scornful. "Maybe pigs'll fly."

"I hope they do. I don't want to spend the rest of my life shouting and yelling at you."

"You don't yell," she paused with one foot in a plastic boot. "You just speak clear. Not like Mr Marshall, and the other teachers. They yell at me all the time. I can't hardly make out a word he says, he runs them all together." She finished putting on her boots. "They think I can't understand. They think I'm thick."

"Never mind them," said Donna, feeling helpless, as she often did. "I bet none of them wrote their first computer programme before they could ride a bicycle."

Al brightened up. "Don't you reckon?"

"Certain. Come on Ali. We must go now, or we'll miss your appointment."

"OK." They left the flat, buttoning their coats against the draught howling up the fire escape and called the lift.

* * *

Kerry was working her way through another hospital day. As a technician, she fitted somewhere in the hierarchy, but the patients seldom knew what to call her. In a place preoccupied with titles and nice distinctions of rank, the most overawed sometimes said 'Doctor' as they hoped for her attention in a long queue. Mostly they settled for 'Miss'.

In audiometry, all was routine. No emergencies were tolerated. Sometimes patients, sick and giddy with middle ear infections would try to be seen before their turn, swooning off the plastic chairs and throwing up on the endless upolished lino. It seldom worked, the hostility of the queue was more of a deterrent than the pain of sitting another hour under the blinking fluorescent lights, not knowing which way was up.

She mended appliances and tested hearing at the behest of the consultant at the smarter end of the wing. The clients would line up, on the rows of uncomfortable seats against the walls of the corridor, if they were lucky enough to find a perch. Out would come their hearing aids for inspection, complaint, repair. Privacy was a luxury that would have required more space and more staff. Neither was available.

"Of course you can't hear anything, Mr Ling." One of her colleagues was yelling at an elderly patient, holding his hearing aid in her hand, scornfully brisk. "You've forgotten to change the batteries." The man, who had thought some new and terrible affliction had deprived him of his last shred of hearing, hung his head.

"I'll get you another battery card, shall I?"

"Uhn," he mumbled, unsure of his volume, but an answer was not required of him.

"And you must remember to check them. Can't have you coming round here every time the batteries run out to get us to change them for you, can we?" The hearing aid was dangled lightly before his eyes, tantalising, withheld to the end of the lecture.

"And don't let the tube get clogged up with wax. See here," the offending part was held close to his face. He squirmed.

"Get the wax out with a matchstick. At least once a day. I'll go and clean it out for you now." The technician walked away. Mr Ling managed to look grateful, hopeful and humiliated all at once.

She saw this scene played out a dozen times a day. Sometimes she heard herself using the same loud bracing tone with patients, praying they wouldn't whine or make a fuss. She had no resources to deal with a constant stream of unhappiness and irritation between nine and five every day. She had become callous. It was with relief she called the next anxious face from the line into the sound booth for a test. She liked this part of the work, the patients safely distant through the thick walls and double windows of the booth. She put tones through their head-phones, noted their response, measured the hearing loss. They could not make any demands of her, the communication was all one way. She looked at the results of the test she was conducting. A falling off at 2000 cycles per second. She could tell the patient herself as she opened the door of the booth, "So high pitched noises you can't hear too well anymore, you'll have to learn to live with it, there's nothing much we can do. Come back in six months if there's any change for the worse." But she said nothing, it was not her part. She would send this one back down to the sunlit office of the consultant, to wait another half hour until he read the notes she had made and announced her conclusions. With suitable gravitas.

"Is that it?" The woman whose hearing she had tested could not believe that such a short exercise could have searched out all her anxiety about deafness.

"That's your lot," she held the door of the sound booth open, pointedly. "Wasn't it worth waiting for?"

"Oh no. I mean yes," worried she may have offended, "though an hour and a half wait for five minutes. . ." She was resentful, but didn't want to push it.

"You're not through yet," Kerry said with a malicious grin. "Off you go back to Mr Entwhistle. He'll want to see you again."

"Will he tell me the results?"

"Yes. You know the way." She stuck her head

round the door and shouted "Next" at the queue, not much caring who responded.

The tired-looking woman at the front of the line nudged the girl beside her to go with Kerry.

"Come along," she snapped leading back to the sound booth. Al followed, with a little wave over her shoulder to Donna, who stayed in her seat.

"Got your appointment card?" Al handed it over while the technician looked quickly at the note the consultant had scribbled in the test-space. This one looks like a stroppy cow, Al thought, noticing the sour tight lines running from the corner of Kerry's mouth to her chin, the way she turned and marched up the corridor as if her shoes had concrete soles.

"OK, in here." She opened the door of the sound booth and ushered the girl in. She started to say "Have a seat," but Al had already jumped onto the stool and picked up the headphones.

"An old hand, eh?" Al grinned at her. Despite the foul mood she was in, and despite her rule about never letting the patients bamboozle her, especially not winsome kids, she smiled back.

"What's your name?" she looked at the card. "Alison is it?"

"That's my proper name."

"What do you get called?"

"Mum calls me Alison, mostly, when she remembers. Or Ali, when she's tired."

"What do your mates call you?"

"Al."

"OK, Al, if you stick those headphones on, like I can see you're about to anyway, I'll go and run the tests."

"What's your name?"

"Kerry."

"Short for anything?"

"No, that's it. Come on, let's get this over with, shall we?"

"Getting worse, aren't I?" Al said, when they had finished.

"The consultant will tell you."

"No he won't. Not if it's Mr Entwhistle. He never

tells me anything. He must think I'm stupid, the way he talks. Like he'd pat my head if he didn't think I had nits."

"I suppose he is a bit patronising."

"He treats me like a child." Kerry was amused by her indignation. "You think it's funny, don't you?" Al accused.

"No I don't." Kerry lied quickly. "But he's like that with everyone, you know. Adults too. He only speaks two languages to the patients – Latin and medical baby-talk."

"Why?"

"He's a bastard."

"But none of you want anyone to know anything. You won't tell me anything."

"Well, I'm a bastard too."

"No, why?"

Kerry sighed. "You're a pest, Al. Nobody tells the patients anything, because the more they know, the more demands they make. It's a load of bother."

"Will you tell me what the results were?"

"I'm not allowed to."

"Be a devil."

"Oh, alright," Kerry capitulated. "Give us your records then. But don't tell anyone, will you? I could get into trouble."

Al sniffed scornfully and handed over the brown envelope which contained her past medical history. Kerry looked through the previous test results.

"You've got a slightly advanced hearing loss in the left ear," she announced. Al nodded. "Satisfied?"

"I knew it anyway."

"You're down for an operation."

"Surprise you?"

"Yes, it does. You don't seem the type."

"Not rich enough, you mean?"

"Yes."

"It's not fair, is it?"

"To those that have, much shall be given," quoted Kerry, piously.

"I don't see why."

"There's a lot of sick people in this country."

"Not surprising either," sniffed Al. "It's like living in a chemical reprocessing plant."

"So if it's a choice between getting some rich businessman back to work, or kitting out an OAP with plastic kneecaps, you can guess which comes first. The businessman's supposed to rush back to his office and start generating wealth, which trickles down to you and me. But where's the profit in granny's new kneecaps? Maybe she spends her last years dancing the hokey-cokey, but she's still going to peg it anyway. What a waste."

"We have to learn that crap at school. The parable of the talents. You don't believe it, do you?"

"No."

"Are you always so sarcastic?"

"Quite often," Kerry confessed. "There's not a lot else I can do, apart from take the piss."

"But what about me? I may not create much wealth, but that don't mean I've no use for my ears."

"Go on, all you common kids want to listen to is that dreadful modern music. Why would they waste an operation on someone who's never even heard of Vivaldi?"

"You're sick, you know that?"

"So my friends tell me."

"If you've got any."

"Charming."

"If you talk to them like you do to me."

"But you're just a patient, hadn't you realised," said Kerry, sweetly. "Shall I tell you what it says in our training manual?"

"I can hardly wait."

"'In the allocation of limited resources, priority must be given to those with higher Social Credit ratings, who, having a higher quality of life in the first place, have the potential, when such a life is extended or improved, to benefit to the full and make a return to the community for its investment.' Unquote."

"You're kidding. Somebody actually said that?"

"Yup."

"And how's someone like me supposed to get a decent Social Credit rating then?"

"Pass exams. Go on young citizenship courses. Join the police cadets."

"Even if you did all that stuff, you still wouldn't have enough. Not if you were really poor to start with."

"I don't actually think the point was to encourage upward mobility. If you want a high rating, you should arrange to be born into a well-off family, and keep both your parents solvent. Otherwise, tough shit."

"It's not fair."

"If I could do anything to change it, I would."

"Would you?" Al eyed her curiously. "Really?"

"Sure. If I knew how."

"There must be a way. If you think about it."

"Let me know if you find one," Kerry said, lightly.

"My mum would say you should get on to your MP. I don't see the point. They're not going to do anything."

"Whoever you vote for, the government always gets elected."

"Nothing changes," Al complained. "It sucks."

"I bet your mother doesn't know you use language like that."

"Oh, don't you start."

"Sorry. Anyway, you're on the waiting list, so I don't know what you're complaining about. The system must have the odd loophole."

Al looked blank. "Must do."

"Good luck to you. God, the rabble will be frothing at the mouth, the time I've spent in here, rabbiting with you." Kerry hustled Al out of the test room and faced the impatient queue.

* * *

Donna tucked her hand firmly through Al's arm and walked along, gripping her daughter above the elbow.

"You don't have to drag me, mum," Al protested. "I still got the use of me legs."

"I'll not have you dawdling along in a dream on your own."

"Where's the fire?"

"We'd miss the bus, if I let you set the pace," Donna sniffed. "I don't like to waste time."

"You never do."

"No thanks to you."

They reached the bus stop. A burly man in a fake sheepskin jacket spat out his chewing gum and pushed his way through the crowd towards them.

"Police." He flapped his warrant card in Donna's face. "Indecency check." Donna stiffened and Al snarled. "You related to the kid?" the man asked, pushing the sunglasses up to the bridge of his nose with a stubby forfinger.

"Of course," Donna answered, looking stolidly at her feet.

"Show me," he demanded. Donna fumbled in her bag for her ID and nudged Al, who dragged her own pass reluctantly out of her pocket. The policeman examined the two bits of plastic, bored, comparing the photos.

"OK." He handed back the identity cards and ambled off.

"Who does he think he is?" Al was indignant. Donna shushed her.

"Why should I be quiet?" Al demanded loudly. "We weren't doing anything wrong."

"He's only checking. It's his job."

"Stupid job. One step down from the sewage works. What a creep."

"Don't be rude," Donna said, sharply. "He doesn't make the laws."

"Who needs it? Laws against holding hands?"

"It's for your own protection."

"I don't need protecting from you."

"Of course you don't, silly. That's why he let us go when he saw I'm your mother."

"I don't need protecting from anyone. Except maybe guys like him."

"Don't be stupid, Alison. There's a lot of nasty people about." Donna looked embarrassed, the bus queue was obviously listening. But she spoke clearly, for Al's benefit. "Perverts. Child molesters. You should be glad the police keep a check on things like that."

"But why check up on women and kids. If it was a man dragging me about, I could understand."

"Perverts are perverts." Donna blushed. "Male and female's all the same to them. They want to bring everyone down to their own level of disease and degradation."

"What do you mean, disease?" Al asked, enjoying the chance to embarrass Donna.

"It's the way they live. I thought they taught you about all that in school."

"The biology teacher does. But she got the sack."

"There you are then." Donna was triumphant. "Quite right too. She was one of them."

"One of what?" Al asked, looking blankly innocent.

"One of those pederasts. It was in the paper."

"She never had a go at any of us." Al was scornful.

"Never got caught maybe." Donna bundled Al onto the bus, which had finally arrived.

"There was a new technician doing my tests. She was OK."

"She looked like a nice girl," Donna agreed.

"That's what you said about the biology teacher when she started at our school," Al reminded her.

"Appearances can deceive."

"They sacked her because of the woman she was living with."

"Quite." Donna plumped into her seat, jamming Al against the window.

"Mum," Al protested. "You're squashing me."

"Sit still then."

"Why shouldn't she?"

"What?"

"Live with a woman?"

"It's unnatural."

"I live with you," Al pointed out reasonably.

"Don't be provocative Alison. You know what I mean."

"No, really. Why shouldn't they?"

"It's wrong." Donna frowned forbiddingly. "Against the laws of god and man. It's a good thing their neighbours reported it. Lucky for all of us there's still some public spirit left."

"I still don't see what's so bad about it."

"You're too young to know." Donna pulled a magazine out of her bag and prepared to close the subject. "Just stay away from that sort. They're disgusting animals." With that, Donna settled down for a comfortable read, leaving Al to stare out of the window.

In his office at Cannon Row, Superintendent Hartley sat waiting for his last meeting of the week to start.

"Do you know, Higgin," he said conversationally to the man seated the other side of his desk, "when I joined the force twenty one years ago, as a hairy-arsed constable, I looked forward to the day when I would have rank, and all its privileges. To sit around behind a desk basking in glory while the lower orders went out and did the leg work. That's how I saw it."

"Sir?"

"And all I do," Hartley continued, as though to himself, "is to go to meetings. And working groups. And consultations. Or worse still," he frowned at Higgin. "Sit around and wait for other bastards to show up, so that meetings can start."

"Yes, sir."

"Which I don't like, Higgin."

"No, sir."

"And what are these meetings about?"

"Sir?"

"Liaison." Hartley spat the word out. "Co-operation. A multi-agency approach to this, and a co-ordinated response to that. No-one commands a squad anymore, they're all falling over themselves to 'head up a unit'. I ask you. Nobody speaks English round here anymore, they all talk in bloody acronyms."

"Yes, sir."

"Three letters used to be considered enough for the average bobby's brain. WPC, SPG, CID, TSG. The ACPO used to stand out as a rarity," he sighed and shook his head. "Not anymore. I don't know why the powers-that-be have such a down on the Masons; their rituals are nothing to the mumbo-jumbo you have to learn in this job. Have you got a degree, Higgin?"

"No, sir." Higgin sat up straight in his chair.

"Good man. You won't get very far, will you?"

"Don't know, sir."

"Take it from me, you won't. I'm a Bachelor of Science. Does that surprise you?"

"Yes, sir," said Higgin, uncertainly, not sure what answer was required.

"I'll take that as a compliment. Complete bloody waste of time it was, but if I hadn't done it, I'd still be a sergeant, like you."

"I'm happy where I am, sir."

"Just a simple country lad, eh? You won't be happy when some jumped-up little inspector ten years your junior starts ordering you around. You get yourself off to college, Higgin. If I could do it, anyone can. Three years of unrelenting slog, surrounded by a filthy horde of poncey unwashed students. A complete and utter waste of time, I don't remember a sodding word of any of the books I read. But all at the taxpayers' expense, and you don't get promotion without a few letters after your name."

"I don't think I'm cut out to be a student, sir."

"I don't doubt it, DS Higgin, not for a moment. Let's just hope that the Banking Societies don't take offence that I've put such an old-fashioned, proud-to-be-an-ignorant-bastard sort of a woodentop on their case."

"No, sir."

"This case," Hartley looked at the report on his desk with distaste. "What's it all about? Computers. Fraud. Three card bloody trickery. I tell you something, Higgin, this sort of caper leaves me cold."

"Sir?"

"I miss the bad old days. When there was real cash money being driven about the country in armour-plated transits, and ordinary blokes with metal cutters and shooters holding them up, while other ordinary blokes with shooters, like me in my Flying Squad days, tried to stop them. Now the poor stupid villains are running errands for snotty suburban drug dealers, who wouldn't know a sawn-off shotgun from a hairdryer; and the poor stupid coppers get sent back to school to learn sociology. Pah! Why did you join the force, Higgin? Not to chase thieves, I hope, or you'd be a disappointed man."

"Oh, you know how it is, sir," said Higgin, diffidently.

"No I don't son, that's why I'm asking you."

"I was working in a garage," Higgin cleared his throat, nervously, "sir. In Bungay. You know the sort of thing, got drunk Friday, played rugby Saturday, slept in front of the telly Sunday afternoon."

"As it is the right of every Englishman to do," intoned Hartley.

Not sure if he was being laughed at, Higgin paused, but the Superintendent waited expectantly, so he continued. "I was just an average sort of a lad; liked a ruck now-and-then, steady money and good mates. Then there was the miners' strike, I was nineteen at the time, and after that Wapping, if you remember, sir?"

"I do indeed."

"Well, it was all on the telly. You saw the police getting stuck in. Nice and simple, it was. Two sides, our lot and theirs, good and bad. So I came up to London and joined the Met."

"To defend democracy?"

"I don't know I'd put it like that, sir," said Higgin, bashfully. "But I did enjoy public order situations. That's what I miss, more than the cash-snatchers, a good public order situation. But of course, you don't get those the same anymore."

"Is that why you got out of uniform?"

"Yes, sir," Higgin's initial reluctance to talk freely to a superior officer was fading fast. "It was getting a bit dull. I thought there might be more crime and less admin work in CID."

"And was there?"

"No, sir. But at least it got me away from domestics and document checks and place-of-safety orders. Bloody social workers, beat officers are now, if you don't mind me saying."

"I'm surprised, with your interest in politics and subversion, that you didn't go into Special Branch."

"I thought about it, sir, but there didn't seem any point. When all the communists had abolished themselves, without so much as a by-your-leave, and the union's got no-strike contracts and seats on the board, what's left? The Irish and the Animal Rights mob. Nothing but grief, the pair of them. So here I am, sir."

"And here I am too," Hartley yawned, "still waiting for this meeting to start. Absolutely bloody typical. Why am I talking to you, Higgin?"

"Don't know, sir," Higgin smiled uncertainly.

"Why am I sitting here, listening to your life story? It's not what I'm paid for, is it?" The Superintendent was suddenly wrathful.

"No, sir."

"So take the bleeding smirk off your face, DS Higgin and go and find where this bloody little man has got to." As Higgin stood up to go, the door was opened by a uniformed constable.

"Mr Letchley to see Superintendent Hartley, sir," he announced, ushering in an average looking man in a business suit. The Superintendent stood up and stretched across his desk to shake hands.

"Glad you could make it, Mr Letchley. Have a seat. This is Detective Sergeant Higgin, who you'll be working with." The two men nodded at each other, Higgin not quite fitting his clothes, still flushed a dull red from lunchtime in the pub; Letchley, paler, thin and tidy, due to start balding in the visible future.

"Sorry to drag you over at such an ungodly time of day," Hartley continued. "But I'm tied up solid next week, and I thought you'd want to crack on."

"It is a matter of some urgency, as far as the Banking Societies Central Security Service is concerned." Letchley's voice was thin and precise. Higgin rolled his eyes to the ceiling and wondered how he was going to share an office with this man.

"And for us. We are pressing on with this enquiry as a priority," Hartley said with smooth insincerity.

"I understand that the police interest arises from investigations into individual cases of Social Security fraud." Hartley nodded agreement. "Cases that were passed on to you for criminal investigation by officials at the Department concerned."

"They point the finger, we dig up the damning evidence," Higgin cheerfully agreed. His superior frowned at the levity. Letchley compressed his narrow lips and carried on, seeming not to notice.

"The Banking Societies, of course, are used to dealing with individual frauds. In this instance, however, there may be a systematic corporate fraud in operation. We believe some of the people you are pursuing in connection with the benefit cases may well be involved, at a low level, with the ability of certain listed organisations to obtain a Credit Transfer Facility."

"Oh yes?" Higgin said, slowly. Despite his exile from Suffolk he still had a slightly agricultural accent.

"The powers that be in the Banking Societies certainly feel it would be a profitable line of enquiry. You naturally will be investigating these individuals suspected of Social Security misdemeanours, we believe the same people may lead us to the perpetrators of a breach in Banking Society security that must worry us all."

"You scratch our back and we'll give you an all over friction rub?" Higgin grinned at him, breathing stale beer fumes. Letchley looked pained.

"Full co-operation has been agreed," Hartley put in quickly. "You'll be based here for a while, Mr Letchley. With DS Higgin as your liaison officer. So you know what we're doing. And vice-versa, of course." Letchley smiled non-committally. "Now, if you'll excuse me, gents," Hartley stood up, the others followed. "I'm sure you'll have a lot to talk about."

By the end of the day, when the last of the patients had been got rid of, even the normally energetic Kerry was tired. She used her weariness as an excuse to avoid going for a drink with the senior technician. As he was her boss, and gently insistent, she usually ran out of plausible excuses about once a week, and had to forfeit a few hours in the bar to him. She suspected that if he hadn't known of her distaste for him, he would not have insisted so often. It was creepy, but at least her department had no night shift. Since his bad report could get her fired, she had to make the best of it.

Standing in line at the staff exit, waiting for her bag to be searched, she was glad to have got away so easily tonight. She pulled her small electric bicycle from the rack and hummed across the car park, an icy wind bringing a chill under her uniform skirt.

The little bike whirred busily along while Kerry debated the relative dangers of being squashed by a lorry on the seething Broadway, or assailed by a mugger in the lonely back streets. To add to her worries, the batteries of her bike gave out on the Hammersmith roundabout walkway. The machine puttered to a halt on the steeply twisting elevated ramp which wound its way round the base of the tower block at the centre of the traffic island. Wondering why powered bikes didn't have pedals for such eventualities, she struggled to push the useless thing home.

The house where she lived with two other women fronted a motorway. It was one of the remnants of a

Victorian terrace, which having subsidence, no foundations and every sort of rot, was unsaleable even by a London estate agent. Perhaps for this reason, its owners had never evicted the occupants, squatters though they were. At least they kept the place from falling down.

Kerry hauled her personal transport up the crumbling steps to the front door, re-locked it behind her and clipped the battery to the recharging point which ran off the illegal mains by-pass.

"Marlene, Ruth. Anyone at home?" Only the cats answered her call, licking their whiskers hungrily. Kerry surrendered to their insistent purring and quickly fed them a tin of minced offal, which described itself as a Rabbit Supreme dinner. She would have preferred a dog, but the feline population had been established long before she moved in, even if they could not do anything useful, like bark.

Only desperate homelessness had led Kerry to contemplate moving into the squat. It was cold, damp and insecure. The neighbours either side, also squatters, were scruffy, anarchic women, whose old radical ethics Kerry considered a back-number. She had been charmed by Marlene, and having nowhere else she could afford to go, had decided to give it a try.

Kerry lit the gas fire in the living room and checked the household computer for messages. The Women's Sound Studio had lost its Credit Transfer Facility, and would have to close down. Kerry swore angrily and retired to the kitchen, to begin peeling onions for tea.

Ruth arrived, fresh from Covent Garden, looking sharp in her business suit. She was a sales manager in advertising. Despite the rigours of the underground, she was well-groomed. The house, which was more prepossessing inside than out, still looked dingy by comparison.

"Hullo, Kerry," she poured herself a glass of water from the fridge. "How are you?"

"Fine," Kerry replied, sweeping crumbs off the kitchen table. "I was wondering how come you always look so piss-elegant in your work clothes?"

"It's my disguise. I go about in the straight world like a spy in occupied territory. What should I wear? Ripped jeans and army boots?"

"You'd probably manage to look as though you were power dressing if you did. What is it with being distinguished, does it come with age?"

"Along with the grey hair and wrinkles. At least I don't have to put them on every day. We're both working-dykes-in-drag, Kerry. You turn out in the morning, the same as I do."

"Except I look like a nice girl and you look impressive."

"It's only a front," Ruth was uncomfortable, unsure how serious this conversation was. She could not always gauge Kerry's moods; they didn't have a lot in common.

Marlene's arrival broke a difficult silence. She was tall and heavily built, in contrast with Ruth's worried-away sort of thinness, she looked solid and sunny. She clumped into the kitchen in frayed jeans and boots, sniffing appreciatively.

"Dinner smells good," she parked herself at the table. "Am I invited?"

"Of course," Kerry put out plates. "I did enough for everyone."

"Here's a woman in keeping with her surroundings," Ruth felt easier now Marlene was present. "The perfect picture of a social outcast. From her unstyled hair to her protruding pink knees. Everything your mother ever told you about squatters here personified."

Marlene looked up with a mouthful and raised her eyebrows interrogatively.

"Kerry doesn't think I'm in my natural habitat," Ruth explained.

"You're not," Marlene agreed. "You look like you should be in a starter home in Uxbridge or a studio flat in Kensal Rise. You made a choice to muck in with the riff-raff. For the likes of me and Kerry, it was all we could get." She chewed contentedly. Ruth looked insulted. Kerry hurried to change the subject.

"I got some bad news about the Women's Sound

Studio today. You'll never guess what the bastards have done to it."

"No parlour games, please," Marlene groaned.

"No, really," Kerry was not much troubled with a sense of humour. "It's dreadful. The Banking Society turned down our application for a Credit Transfer Facility."

"Surprise, surprise," Ruth yawned.

"'It is the considered opinion of the manager of this branch that it would be unsafe and unsound to issue a Credit Transfer Facility to your enterprise as it is presently constituted,'" murmured Marlene.

"Yes, the usual stuff," Kerry agreed impatiently.

"The Friendly One, was it?"

"Yes, but they're all the same. No point trying any others, now we've been listed."

"You never stood a chance in the first place," Ruth said.

"They gave us a temporary facility. We had a Credit Transfer machine," Kerry bristled. "They came and took it away this afternoon."

"You only got it because you didn't tell them it wasn't a mixed, commercial studio you were setting up," Ruth was dismissive.

"It was worth a try. But what are we going to do now?"

"Busk," said Ruth, unfeelingly.

"Ruth, it may have escaped your notice, but in a cashless society, there is bugger all point in busking. What's the audience supposed to throw into the hat? Peanuts? IOUs? If we don't have a Credit Transfer Facility, there's no way anyone can get money from their Banking Society account to ours."

"Really?" Ruth was sarcastic. "Makes you wonder what happened to the guy who used to play the bagpipes in Oxford Street."

"If he had friends like you to help him out, he probably died of starvation."

"You could always sell your trombone."

"Are you serious?" Kerry was outraged.

"No, actually I was making a joke. You remember them?"

"I don't think it's a laughing matter," said Kerry, stiffly.

"Obviously."

"It's not just me, though god knows where the band is going to rehearse. Lots of women use the place."

"Ah, but for what? Romantic liaisons, so I hear."

"Don't be too hard on them," scolded Marlene. "You know musicians can't help their passionate natures."

"Maybe they could re-apply as a dating agency, or a sex therapy centre. Therapy's very bankable."

"You may not think that music is revolutionary enough," sniffed Kerry. "But the government, or whoever decides about Credit Transfer obviously does. Otherwise they wouldn't be closing us down."

"Oh, it's powerful stuff, I agree," Ruth hummed a few bars of the European anthem. "But I've seen a lot of women's organisations forced to close down for want of a Credit Transfer Facility. And I'm not personally involved in this one, like you are."

Kerry, who had hoped for a more sympathetic response to her news, dumped the washing-up in the sink and considered her strategy.

"I was wondering. . ." she began.

"Wonder no more," Ruth interrupted. "The answer is no."

"You know what I was going to ask?"

"It doesn't strain my powers of intuition."

"Give the woman a chance," Marlene mediated in her usual easy-going way.

"I hoped your group would be able to do something for the Sound Studio," Kerry addressed herself to Ruth.

"It isn't my group," Ruth looked implacable. "And I thought you weren't interested in it anyway. Too dangerous or something, wasn't it?"

"I did some work for you," Kerry was indignant. "Who was it who hacked her way into the customer vetting section of the Friendly One, when you lost access to your old Banking Society?"

"And since then, what?" demanded Ruth. "You lose interest and the rest of us have to slog on with the hard work and risk of fixing up arrangements for women with no Credit Transfer Facility. In our spare time, which is every bit as precious as yours, while you always have more interesting things to do than help."

"We did hope you would be more involved," Marlene said, tugging the curtains across the draughty window-frame. "After all, you seemed to take to the work very easily."

"Is that why you asked me to live here?" Kerry inquired bitterly. "To recruit another drone for the Credit Transfer group?"

"I suggested you move in," Marlene explained, "because you were seriously homeless and I thought we could all get on."

Ruth raised her lightly plucked eyebrows impatiently. "Nobody forced you," she said. "I don't care if you want in or out of the Credit Transfer group, so long as you don't think you can use us when you need us, without putting in any effort of your own."

"For Christ's sake," Kerry snapped, "I only asked if you could do something for the Women's Sound Studio, so they don't have to close down."

"But Kerry," Marlene bent all her co-counselling skills to the task of achieving harmony, "there are dozens of women's organisations waiting for our services. You must realize that we can't drop everything to help the studio. Especially if you won't share the work."

"Shape up or ship out," snapped Ruth, tiring of the argument. "I'm going to have a bath." She stalked off.

Marlene smiled ruefully at Kerry. "I wouldn't put it so bluntly, but you should listen to what she's saying."

"Meaning what?"

"That the trade-off for us fixing up something for the Sound Studio is that you have to become more involved in the work of the group."

"What if I don't want to?" Kerry demanded.

"It would take that much longer for us to be able to help them. Anyway, you were good at setting these things up, when you tried it. . ."

"Briefly, you should say."

"I wasn't going to. You and Ruth both seem to find it so easy, breaking into a database. Computers aren't an effort for either of you, like they are for me."

"Should I be flattered?"

"We all have our different talents. It would be good if you were to become more committed to the group."

"Don't start talking to me about commitment," Kerry pulled a face. "I get enough of that from Ruth. In fact, I think I prefer having my arm twisted by her. At least she doesn't have to be nice about it. But you can tell her and the girls next door that I'll rejoin your criminal conspiracy. I don't have any choice, do I?" she finished, petulantly. "So now will you tell me the current password?"

Marlene laughed. "You look cute when you pout, did you know that?"

Kerry did not want to know. Cuteness was not the effect she aimed for. She had hoped, when Marlene had offered her the place, that it was more than her potential commitment that the big woman was after. If Marlene was aware of this interest, she did not let on. Kerry had mistaken the friendliness and concern for something more personal, until she realised that Marlene was generally friendly and concerned. Not like Ruth, who couldn't have cared if you came off a production line, so long as you were involved in one of her various good causes.

Kerry had subsequently convinced herself that Marlene was not, anyway, her type. She was imposingly large and always scruffy. She looked more like a dyke than Kerry considered safe. She was dangerously obvious to other women, and obviously dangerous to men. She had no apparent means of support, apart from the minimal Income Assistance that was credited to her account every month. Kerry wondered whether Ruth subsidised her, or whether Ruth's brand of charity would be directed at organisations rather than individuals.

"It will be nice to have you working with us again," Marlene broke in on her reverie. "It might make things easier in the house as well."

"Wishing you had never invited me?"

"Not at all. It's just you and Ruth could do with being more co-operative."

"I don't have the right attitude, as far as she's concerned," Kerry sneered.

"Sweetheart, nobody cares about your attitude, so long as you set up those false companies and get them cleared for use. Ruth does it because of her politics, me, I just like to help out. You can do it because you think you ought to, or because it's a challenge, or even because Ruth bullied you back into it. I don't suppose the women we assist will bother about your motivation."

"I'll never be as dedicated as Ruth, she's got a monopoly on that. And I don't want to be like her when I'm in my thirties – busting a gut over the day job and then coming home to endless struggle. Whoever heard of a revolutionary sales manager?" Kerry suddenly realised that as Marlene was at least as old as Ruth, she might have been tactless, and blushed.

"Oh, it's good she's keeping active, don't you think?" Marlene teased. "At her age?"

"You and Ruth are like oil and vinegar," Kerry exclaimed. "You're so calm and she's always angry. By rights you shouldn't mix."

"Maybe it's because we've got you to shake us up." Unsure what to make of this, Kerry chewed her nails in silence. Her ears stuck out from the side of her head and she even had a dimpled chin. Marlene could not help finding her cute. She didn't mention it again.

"Well," Kerry said at last, "If I'm going to save the Women's Sound Studio, I'd better get on with it. If Ruth comes down, make her day, tell her I'm doing some work."

* * *

Behind the hotel was a courtyard, walled in and sheltered. A ramp led down to the basement goods delivery bay. The front of the hotel was grand and towered over Mayfair, but the rear was quiet and a good place to sleep.

The woman had not arrived in time to secure a place next to the metal vents which provided an outlet for the heating system. Even if she had, it wasn't worth the trouble. All through the night, newcomers would challenge for the warm spots. It was only sensible to settle there if you could fight off all comers. She had seen a man blinded with a broken bottle for daring to sleep in the place another tramp considered rightfully his.

Arriving as it grew dark, she made her bed of flattened cardboard and packaging material in the far corner of the yard, by the entrance from the street. A man of indeterminate age, wearing a skirt, or a kilt, tried to share his bottle of cleaning fluid with her, but she refused with a grunt and an off-putting stare.

The smell of cooking hung about the basement windows and rose up into the yard through the metal grilles on which sleepers lay. The woman dribbled a trickle of saliva. She was not aware of drooling, the feeling in that side of her face had not fully returned after the last-but-one ride in a police van, during which her nose had been broken.

Two teenage absconders, skinny boys in thin black clothes, dossed down in her corner of the yard. She resented the intrusion, but they giggled and offered her a drag on the cigarette they were sharing. Ignoring her unwelcoming air, they made themselves comfortable, though not as expertly as she had done.

It was past midnight and everyone was fitfully asleep or anaesthetised, when the vigilantes burst into the yard. Four young men, army trousers tucked into their long boots, leather jackets, paratroopers' berets. Sunglasses, even in the night. The concrete floor magnified the noise of their clubs banging on the closed rubbish skip. Some of the less bleary scrambled to their feet, but the only exit was blocked.

Without speaking, the crew laid about them, bludgeoning the men and women in the yard with baseball bats. One stood guard in the gateway as the other three waded into the sleepers by the vents, aiming blows across elbows and knees.

"Mind the blood," cautioned the largest vigilante,

as they dragged the two boys out of the corner. "They're druggies."

"Fucking renters," one of them smashed the white-faced boy over the head. His friend was transfixed. "Diseased scum." He knocked the other one to the ground and began kicking him in the stomach. The rest of the gang gathered round the two boys on the floor. The old woman curled up in her corner, squeezing her eyes tightly shut. She heard the thumping of boots against bodies for what seemed like an eternity. One of the boys screamed, then whimpered and finally was silent. The older vagrants were picking themselves up if they could and creeping out of the yard, past the preoccupied men. One of the gang unbuttoned his trousers and pissed on the boy lying at his feet. As he finished, shaking himself nonchalantly, a police car drove slowly past, searching with its spotlight. Without hurrying, the four men straightened their berets and strolled out into the street. If the policemen saw their clubs gleaming wetly in the spotlight, and connected it with the blood trickling across the pavement into the gutter, they did nothing about it.

When everyone else who could walk had gone, the woman sadly folded her bedding into plastic bags and came out of the corner. She passed the two boys, lying in a sodden heap. Neither of them was dead, she thought, but there was nothing she could do. She was sorry for them, but the blood which oozed from them was certainly alive with one of the twenty seven strains of Human ImmunoDeficiency Virus, and she had no intention of dabbling in it. One of the boys opened his eyes as she shuffled past, stopping her in her tracks. For some reason, she didn't want them to see her deserting them. Even with his eyes open, the boy's mangled face showed no signs of consciousness, and presently she left them there alone.

Detective Sergeant Higgin burst into his office at 9.45 am with all the rancorous exhaustion of a man who has been up half the night with a baby vomiting down the front of his pajama jacket.

Letchley was already there, working at a table that had been filched from the canteen, squeezed in between Higgin's own desk and the door. He was in shirt sleeves, his jacket suspended tidily on a coat-hanger he had brought with him on his second day.

"Fucking babies." Higgin slung his own jacket over the back of his chair and put a plastic mug of coffee down precariously on a heap of papers and directories on his desk.

"Good morning." Letchley barely looked up. "Children still poorly?"

"Little bleeders." Higgin slumped into his chair and fished a matchstick out of the over-full ashtray. Letchley watched in silent horror as he wiped the matchstick, split it in two and began digging breakfast out from between his teeth. "Didn't get a wink. Anything up?"

"Records say the last batch of personal files on the Social Security frauds are temporarily unavailable."

"Lost the buggers? Oh well." Higgin finished picking his teeth, drank his coffee, crumpled the cup and threw it in the general direction of the waste bin in the corner. A wet brown trail of coffee drops splattered across Letchley's table. Taking a tissue from his pocket, he carefully dried the mess and put the tissue in the bin, along with the cup which had landed beside it.

"That would seem to be so."

"Always happening. So much for the increased efficiency of computerised records."

"An automated record system should be more efficient."

"In the old days, you see, all the records actually existed. In the real world, on grubby bits of paper."

"The good old days?" put in Letchley, eyebrow raised.

"Damn right. Well, when they lost things then, you could swan down to records and give some runty little copper a right bollocking, so he'd trot off and dig it up for you, they always had to be somewhere. Now if you can find anyone in records at all, it'll be some supercilious git with a BTEC in computing, telling you the file you want's disappeared in an electro-magnetic hiccup somewhere down the line between here and Hendon. And there's never anything you can actually get your hands on."

"Ah, the reassurance of the tactile reality," Letchley smiled.

"Come again? Second thoughts, don't bother. Anyway, it's a good thing I kept my notes." Higgin sat back with a smug look.

"Some of the first cases were interesting," Letchley mused. "Those women in Talgarth Road, the squatters. There appears to be quite a coven of them."

"Failure to repay Lifeline loans. Suspect Income Assistance claims. Bunch of dykes, if you ask me. All bloody girls together. There's a reference to Special Branch on a couple of them, if we're going to pull them in."

"I think you should. They do sound promising and there seems to be enough leverage there to persuade at least some of them to be forthcoming."

"You just want the commercial frauds, don't you?"

"That's right."

"Why don't we have a trawl through this bunch, pick out the most likely prospects and get the Special Branch to give us the groups they're involved with? So when we're leaning on them, we know the answers we're looking for. Makes it quicker."

"It sounds a sensible approach."

"Good. Then that's what we'll do." Higgin picked up the phone and asked for warrants. Letchley stood up and eased himself sideways through the space between his table and the wall. "White, two sugars, if you're going," said Higgin, without looking up.

By the time the answer to Higgin's query came hissing off the printer the afternoon was dying on its feet. The four o'clock aspirin rush, when the headaches born of bad light, bad air and thin walls got a grip, had hit the first aid box as usual. Higgin dropped a copy of the list of names and affiliations in front of his temporary colleague.

"There you go."

"Good." Letchley began reading eagerly, checking the names against a list of his own.

"Fancy a drink?" Higgin sat on the edge of Letchley's table, swinging a leg and trying to read upside down.

"A bit early, isn't it?" Letchley looked up, irritated. All his things were neatly laid out on his table, it was obviously his marked territory. And Higgin was sitting on it, looming over him, making his hackles rise. A suspicion that the East Anglian policeman was being deliberately oafish crossed his mind.

"Go on," Higgin pressed, "you do drink, don't you?"

"Oh alright."

"Bring the list, will you?" Higgin grinned at him. "In case you start pining for your work."

"Hardly likely." Letchley was shaking his jacket from its hanger and putting it on.

"No, go on. I didn't get a chance to look at it properly yet."

"Very well." Letchley took the list and some other papers from his desk and snapped them into his infobag on top of the small portable computer.

They left Cannon Row and jostled through the crowd of evening commuters and tourists to the pub. It was full of policemen in civvies, but neither of them minded that. Higgin liked being around other coppers, when he wasn't home with the family, and Letchley had the manner of a naturalist seeing a strange breed in its original habitat.

Letchley surprised Higgin by going straight to the bar and asking for a scotch, raising an eyebrow for Higgin's order. A pint. He gave the barman his credit card, looked closely at the till debit slip that came back with it. Such a dry looking little man, thought Higgin. He still didn't know him any better, even after being cooped up in the same office for days. Finicky, he was, obsessively tidy. A bit superior in his manner. Made it plain he found the station, with its constant scrum of harassed, cursing policemen, inefficient. An anachronism he'd called it, the first day, though Letchley was one of those himself, with his two piece suit and raincoat, his shoes always shined and the borrowed hair combed across his thin patch.

"Cat got your tongue?" Letchley watched him, obviously troubled with the effort of thought.

"Sorry, mate. I was miles away. Cheers." He took a great gulp of beer.

"Cheers."

"Come on then. What's the starting price?" Higgin demanded.

"I beg your pardon?"

"You're not being straight with me, Mr Letchley. You have information about these groups you're after which you haven't shared with me in a frank and comradely manner. In a word you're not telling me all you know. And I want the lowdown."

"Oh."

"Yes, 'oh'. I know you think all policemen have room for three short planks and not much else between their ears. And I'm a bumpkin to boot in your book. But I'm not such a fool as you take me for."

"I don't."

"So come on," Higgin enjoyed having made Letchley uncomfortable. "Your boss didn't set all this up just so you could meet interesting hunky members of the old bill and broaden your social horizons. You must have something to go on. Spill the beans."

"There's nothing definite."

"You weren't interested in any of our villains except those women from Talgarth Road."

"They look very likely targets."

"I reckon you were looking out for them from the start."

"Not necessarily those particular individuals."

"But something like it?"

"Yes." Letchley poured half a bottle of ginger ale into his scotch, letting the bubbles tickle his nose. "I have been less than forthcoming, I suppose. But it was my superiors' choice that I should be circumspect, at this stage, not my own."

"He's only doing his job," Higgin mocked.

"It is a delicate position, you must appreciate. What we are working on is gossip and unsubstantiated rumour. Most regrettable."

"The stuff of which prosecutions are made," said Higgin cynically.

"My boss put out feelers to your top brass and when the benefit cases came in, with a batch of our possibles in there, we were tipped off. Here I am."

"But those women," Higgin was incredulous, "they're never masterminding a corporate fraud?"

"Not in themselves, no. But I believe they may be the legmen, as you would call it," Higgin groaned, but Letchley failed to notice, "of a larger organisation. A committed group of revolutionaries undermining the whole basis of financial security."

"Well, fuck me." Higgin slapped his well padded thigh.

"Perhaps I get a little carried away," Letchley restrained himself severely. He laid two sheets of printout on the table, having looked quickly round the smoky room to check that none of the other customers in the pub were doing more than getting drunk from the office and making themselves late home to their wives.

"What's this then?"

"Read them."

The first listed the groups in which Special Branch knew the benefit suspects to be involved. The second was a memo to Letchley from the head of his section at the Banking Society, marked "Strictly Confidential". It listed some twenty organisations: refuges; centres; co-ops; holiday homes; bookshops and clubs. Most of the names began with Women's this or Women's that.

"So?"

"The second list is what my department is working on. Women's organisations who were refused Credit Transfer Facilities which, it is alleged, are still functioning. Thriving, even," he said bitterly, seeming to take it as a personal affront. "If you look at the suspect group of women on the first list, your own Special Branch report, you will notice that there is some overlap. All of the women seem to have been involved with at least one of the organisations which we have tried to put out of action. As the Home Office wished us to, I might add. In confidence."

"Sure," Higgin murmured, frowning over the two lists. "But if they've got a scam like this going, it must be a huge moneyspinner. Why are they bothering with poxy little benefit rip-offs?"

"Criminals can be very stupid, I believe. But I doubt whether these are central characters. An organised gang must be behind it and, no doubt, keep most of the profits."

"So what are these small-time slags up to?"

"I think they must have been necessary points of contact with the women's centres and so on. Obviously, some professional criminal has devised a system whereby listed organisations may obtain a Credit Transfer Facility. And since many subversive women's organisations were among the first to be listed, they decided to target them as customers for their services. These women," he tapped the police list, "must have been used as an entrée to that shady world."

"You reckon?"

"That is the theory on which I am working." Letchley carefully retrieved the two papers and stored them again in his infobag, spinning the combination locks. Higgin watched him with a mixture of doubt and amusement.

"Who decides that an organisation gets the big raspberry and has its CT machine taken away?"

"There is a central committee in which all the Banking Societies participate. That's public knowledge."

"And the Home Secretary?"

"Any representations he might make about the unsuitability of certain organisations would naturally be taken into consideration. But the primary judge ment is a financial one. If a concern cannot demonstrate that it is a proper organisation, with probity and respect for the conventions of financial control, then Credit Transfer Facilities are refused."

"Simple."

"Indeed."

"And of course, most of the people subverting the state just don't happen to have a lot of probity. Whatever that is."

"Certainly not."

"There you go then."

"There were far too many women's things around," Letchley mused, "a legacy of the permissive society, I've always felt."

"My wife's in the townswomen's guild. Think I should tell her they'll be listed for subversives?" Higgin teased.

"Of course not. You know what I mean. Those organisations that were, are, aggressively anti-men. They're all lesbians you know."

"Never!"

"You may laugh now, DS Higgin, but if you'd read some of their literature. I can tell you, it's blood curdling. The things they'd do, if only they could get themselves organised."

"Lucky for us they can't."

"It is indeed."

"Beats me why any bloke with the gumption to get fake Credit Transfer Facilities should waste his time messing about with a bunch of hags like that."

"Money. There would be a lot in it. And this is only one group of clients we have identified. There must be many others. Think what you could charge for a service like that." Letchley's eyes gleamed. "And once the system was established, the returns would represent almost pure profit, I imagine. No tax or other overheads, which so inhibit most new enterprises. Even if they're only charging a flat fee, rather than a percentage of turnover, which would be quite feasible, they must be raking it in. They have their clients over a barrel."

"Ah well, you'll have to put a stop to that, won't you?"

"Yes," Letchley sighed wistfully. "It would be something for my career, you know. A coup such as that."

"Wouldn't do mine any harm, I daresay," said Higgin slowly.

"You know," Letchley was off on his own, "sometimes I feel that my career is stagnating. I don't know why. I've made all my promotions on schedule. It's something I can't pin down."

"Sounds like a bad case of 'what's it all for' to me," Higgin punched the other man gently on the forearm, making him start.

"Oh no. I know what it's for. I have no doubt in my mind on that score."

Higgin raised his glass. "To catching villains. And promotion." Letchley drank with him and almost smiled.

* * *

"You did what?" Kerry shouted. "You said we would provide a Credit Transfer Facility for a brothel?"

"Keep your voice down," Marlene hushed, "Ruth will hear."

"I didn't suppose you had told her. You must be crazy."

"Please Kerry. Just do it for me."

"Why the hell should I? I'm not a pimp."

"I promised." Marlene chewed her lip.

"Are they paying you?" Kerry had never seen Marlene so agitated.

"No. I met this woman, Lynette. She's Trish's sister. If they don't get a Facility, they'll all be out on the streets."

"So what?"

"So they'd be dead inside three months."

"That's no reason for you to get involved."

"Some of them are dykes," Marlene persuaded, keeping an eye on the living room door in case Ruth should appear.

"I don't care," Kerry shrugged, "it's men who benefit if you set them up."

"Kerry, I'm not asking you to like it. Just don't tell the others."

"It's a ridiculous risk to take."

"We take them all the time," Marlene argued.

"This isn't exactly a women's group, is it? No wonder you don't want the others to know."

"Ruth would only say that they were propping up patriarchy," Marlene protested.

"For once I might have to agree with her."

"But they don't have any other options." Marlene tried again. "Please, Kerry. Get me a line to the Banking Society, so I can input their new identity. It's only a one-off."

"Too right it is," Kerry stopped pacing up and down, and looked at Marlene. "If I give you a hand, it's only to stop you messing it up and getting us caught."

"Thanks, Kerry. I'm really grateful."

"I must be getting as soft as you are," Kerry complained, sitting down at the computer.

Al lay on her bed sucking the blood from her knuckles, watching the lights from the flyover reflected on the ceiling. She was alone in the flat, in the dark with the vibration of a heavy-footed row next door coming through the walls.

She looked at her hand. It had almost stopped bleeding. A dark, sluggish ooze, with flaps of torn skin sticking out of the clotting mess. She put her fist back in her mouth and sucked thoughtfully. It tasted alright. The saltiness surprised her.

It was late. She decided to get cleaned up before Donna got in. Her mum didn't like fighting. Al rolled off her bed and went to the tiny bathroom. Reluctantly she rinsed away the lumps of thickened blood and scabbing, watching them slip to the bottom of the basin in sticky streamers washed down the plug with a trickle of hot water. She poured disinfectant onto cotton wool and dabbed at the drying cuts, enjoying the sting and the way white tufts of cotton stuck to the punctures in her skin. She wondered if gangrene looked like that, when you let a cut go mouldy; like old bread with whiskers.

She finished up, stuck on plasters that immediately began unwrapping themselves around the knuckle and went to make herself a sandwich. She was meant to cook something, there was a tin of stew, but she couldn't be bothered. The lumps of meat, with their attachments of fat and globs of gravy, reminded her too much of how the inside of a cut looked anyway.

They had crept up behind her, standing at the bus stop, waiting to come home from school. Three of them, they took it in turns to come up close behind her and whisper things in her ear. Her left ear, they knew that was the worst, they would whisper things so she couldn't hear. But she knew they were doing it, not what they were saying. It was a game of grandmother's footsteps, only not a game to her.

Danny Morgan and his cousin Wayne. With Cyndi in tow. She would never forgive Cyndi. Never speak to the little cow again. She knew how much Al would hate it. Knew, though the other two only guessed. She had spun round and seen their faces, Danny's leering grin, Wayne practically wetting himself with enjoyment. And Cyndi, looking pleased and guilty and proud to think she was one of the lads, one of the gang. Maybe she suggested it, even, to get in with them. The others weren't doing anything about it, in the bus queue, standing watching, laughing or bored, the older ones pretending they weren't amused, taken up with smoking and flirting with each other.

Danny dodged round behind her, when she turned, and murmured something in her ear. She could feel the buzz of his lips among her hair. Wayne's face split open, he squirmed with laughter. Great yuks and bellows of noise came at her. Danny was saying some filth, she could guess. He would write obscenities on the bus shelter, so they had to look at it every day and have him think they were getting off on reading his graffiti, or avoid looking at it, and let him know he had made them uncomfortable.

Every time she turned, Danny skipped around behind her again and said something for the benefit of Wayne and Cyndi that she couldn't hear. They would go on till the bus came. She knew that everyone was waiting to see what she would do.

Wayne's grinning face came within reach and she shot out a fist at his gaping mouth. She felt teeth move satisfyingly against her knuckles, saw the blood start from his gums like a red mouth-wash.

She spun round and caught Danny a hard kick on the side of the knee. He swiped at her, but without force, his balance disturbed. She brought her own knee sharply up to hit him where the nerves ran down beside the thigh bone. His leg went dead and he toppled slowly over. Wayne was crying, dribbling blood down his chin, holding a slimy incisor, not knowing what to do with it. In the end he put it in the pocket of his jeans, unwilling to believe he had been permanently separated from it. Danny was trying to get up, swearing at her and surprised. But she had turned for Cyndi, grabbed her by hair and wrist, butting furiously with her forehead at the other girl's nose, wanting blood for her treachery.

A couple of the older boys, who had watched her flatten Wayne and Danny with superior amusement, now wrenched Cyndi from her grip. They didn't like to see girls fighting with each other. Cyndi ran off, gulping tears and snot. Al stood, white faced and shaking, clutching a fistful of torn hair.

"Fucking interfering bastard." The boy who held her shoulders while Cyndi was prised from her, laughed. Wayne and Danny had slunk away, more humiliated than hurt.

No-one sat next to her on the bus, but then no-one usually did anyway. She was accustomed to being different. She had friends, some friends, she was tough. She wondered when she would get used to people imitating her strangely pitched voice and laughing at her, and to the way her damaged hearing kept the world at half-arms length from her.

Waiting for her mum to get in from work that night, she decided she wouldn't tell her about the fight. Donna would say it took two sides to make a quarrel. She reckoned if anybody provoked you, there were two things you could do. Reason with them, or take no notice. Definitely not smack them in the teeth. Al had been brought up to believe that all bullies were cowards and that a soft answer turns away wrath. Experience had soon taught her otherwise, but she kept the discovery to herself.

She got up and wandered over to her computer. It was cheap, and five years out of date, but quite powerful. She booted up and started writing a game programme. Her graphics fx were limited, but with a bit of ingenuity she could send Cyndi and Danny and Wayne running round and round a maze on her screen, while her cursor waited in cul-de-sacs to gobble them up. She could make them scurry around one of her games helpless to defend themselves from the gobbling blobs and rockets she sent after them. This time, she didn't bother writing any sound fx into the programme.

Between Baron's Court and West Kensington, single occupancies were rare. The large terraced houses had been divided, re-developed and gutted, until five or more studio flats could be squeezed behind each street door. Number 12, Athene Road, with only two buzzers on the entryscan, was unusual.

In better days, the top buzzer had connected to Madame's flat. A disagreement with the Inland Revenue, who had no scruples about living off immoral earnings, had removed Madame temporarily to a privately run prison in Sussex. Although there was no-one living over the shop, productivity in the lower part of the building was maintained.

Carole and Lynette were having a smoke in the lobby, counting the days until Madame could get paroled. The complications of running an unlicensed small business were a burden, but there was no alternative. Three other women were upstairs with clients. None of them had ever had outdoor work, nor did they wish to try it. If they weren't free from the risk of murderous vigilantes, seropositive men with revenge in mind, or the insatiable demand for freebies from every sort of government official, at least they could get paid. You couldn't tuck a Credit Transfer machine in your suspender belt and loiter on York Way. Street girls and boys could only barter their bodies for drugs. Carole and Lynette both planned to retire with something in the Banking Society.

The entryscan blinked. Carole activated the microphone.

"Who is it," she inquired, although she recognized the face on the screen.

"Henry," his voice crackled back, confirming his

identity. She pressed another button and heard the deadbolt snap back on the front door.

"It's that sweaty Detective Constable from Shepherd's Bush," Carole complained. "He'll want it without a rubber."

"Silly sod," Lynette stood up. She heard the crash of breaking glass and saw the stun grenades hurtling through the broken window. The blast was like the time her husband had kicked her in the head, then jumped on her stomach. He couldn't have afforded the abortion, or the loss of her earnings, so he locked her in the bathroon until she finished miscarrying. Lynette felt the same now, lying on the floor, unable to think or move.

Men who looked like space workers tore through the house kicking open every door. Their protective suits of gleaming silver polytripropide were topped by face masks and helmets. Their steps, although heavy, were muffled by white rubber boots. Lynette and Carole had their hands lashed behind them with plastic cable and were dragged, still dazed, to their feet. Nobody spoke. One of the women being hauled downstairs was epileptic – the stun grenades had started her fitting. It took three policemen to carry her out. The other two girls, and the men who had been with them, were brought out, undressed and bound.

Blood samples were taken from them at the holding centre. Lynette sweated out the day waiting for the results. If one of them was positive, it would be attempted murder, and the rest of them charged as accessories before the fact. Carole, in the other cell, sweated even more. She had been through a forced withdrawal before, and knew she could not bear it again. Her anti-body status did not concern her, although she had shared the works often enough.

Carole's trembling distress had been well observed. She was left overnight, the last to be questioned. The burly Detective Constable, whom she knew better without his clothes on, interviewed her several times over the week of her detention. Carole had no loyalty, except to herself. The possibility of bail persuaded her to assist with inquiries. She could have been more helpful – Carole had never been good at remembering names and, as time passed, panic increased her incoherence. It was when her interrogators were attempting, for the fifth time, to discover who had supplied a Credit Transfer Facility to the brothel, that Carole collapsed.

"She practically pegged it," Higgin complained. "Right there in the interview room. Stroke. I ask you, she was only twenty five."

"Drug abuse," Letchley nodded, "collapsed veins, thrombosis, detached clots. Nasty business. Did she survive?"

"She's alive, but no use. Can't talk."

"What a nuisance," Letchley tapped rapidly at the keys of the office terminal as he talked, not needing to watch what he was doing. Higgin had a grudging admiration for his dexterity. "And just when they had got to the interesting part."

"From what the DC who interviewed her tells me, he had already got to the interesting part with Carole," Higgin leered, "and it wasn't anything to do with Credit Transfer."

"I'm sure," Letchley blinked. "What could she tell him?"

"Some woman set it up for them. When the tax people busted the place and they had to get a new Credit Transfer identity. She told Carole her name was Lee, but I don't suppose it was. She couldn't remember where the contact lived, but thought it was somewhere local. Carole said this woman was a lesbian."

"Would she know?"

"Carole? She wasn't one herself, if that's what you mean."

"I thought prostitutes often were," Letchley mused. "You'd think it would give them a distaste for their work."

"Who cares if they like it?" Higgin gave him a sour look.

"I'd call Talgarth Road local, wouldn't you?" Letchley continued smoothly. "Not far from Carole's place of work at all."

"Just round the corner," Higgin agreed, finding it on the wall map of London. "Why?"

"These women in the squats," Letchley cracked his knuckles one by one. "Another shred of circumstantial evidence, don't you think?"

"But this isn't political," Higgin protested. "It's a knocking shop. I don't see that it's got anything to do with your conspiracy theory. Keeping whores in trade isn't going to start the women's revolution."

"Maybe those women are committed to political activity," Letchley theorized, "but they have become involved with a gang whose only interest is profit. Whatever their moral stance might be, I am sure those in charge expect them to keep delivering new clients."

"I'm not convinced."

"It's a possibility. One must keep an open mind."

"I think you're pissing in the wind," Higgin said, rudely. "I'm not even sure these women we're pulling in for you have anything to do with it."

"We'll see," Letchley was unperturbed. "It's one more angle to try when we have them in."

* * *

When Kerry decided to go out for the evening, it was already late. She was tired when she got in from the hospital. Then she'd had to put in a few hours on the Women's Sound Studio's new fake commercial identity. She wanted to sleep for a week, so perversely she threw on her coat and headed east, uptown.

Anything to get away from Ruth and Marlene and the rest of the gang. They'd all come clomping into the living room as she was finishing off her feminist chore for the evening. Ruth had smiled to herself at the sight, pleased at the success of her strategy for getting Kerry back into the fold.

She buzzed through Knightsbridge on her electric bicycle and into Hyde Park. Past the building site, which would be another luxury hotel when it grew up. Marlene had pointed it out to her as the place where she had stood and listened to speeches, when she used to go on marches. That had been ten or more years ago. People still organised marches occasionally, but no-one went on them anymore. The police always gave you a route from Redbridge to Barking, down the backstreets and on a Sunday, as the only possibility for a licence. Nobody got within spitting distance of parliament wearing a badge or carrying a banner, these days. No demonstrations within five miles of the Palace of Westminster, in session or out.

She was quite pleased with the cover she was making for the Studio. She'd lost none of her skill. It had to be something in a similar line, so the credits and debits wouldn't be from hopelessly incompatible sources. She had created an instrument and p.a. hire firm called Budget Sounds. Nice and bland. There was a time when she'd had to stop them all inventing names like "Sapphic Stores" and "Battleaxe Bikes". Stuck out a mile.

She slid into the Marble Arch pedestrian underpass, the little bike's brakes whining down the steep gradient. The concrete was wet, the drains running full. The dossers and tramps must just have been hosed out of the shelter of the tunnel. Kerry emerged into Green Street, riding illegally across the pavement.

Maybe Ruth and Marlene were sleeping together. It surprised her that she hadn't thought about it before. They were thick as thieves lately. No wonder she felt excluded. Even if they weren't lovers, they were certainly starting to act like a couple. Bad news in a house of three. Bad news in any house, come to think of it. Although she had known Marlene over a year, she could not understand her taste in women. Ruth was so abrupt. Marlene, easy going and warm, had the confidence based on her strength which lay so easily in her long, solid limbs and back. Kerry sighed. Marlene's body hair was reddish gold, she looked sleek in the morning sunlight. She had a big crooked smile, improbably white teeth and her room was full of thriving house-plants which never died or got the blotchy mould. How could you not fall for a woman like that?

Off the back of Oxford Street, on the edge of Soho, she chained her bicycle to a set of railings, padlocked the battery and removed the leads.

Down the area steps she went, to the basement of the blank and peeling old building. She rang the buzzer beside the heavy barred door and the video camera winked into life. She turned her face towards where she knew the lens to be, so the door keeper wouldn't leave her standing in the cold all night. A hatch in the door opened and a hand shot out, smooth with a heavy metal ring on the little finger.

"Membership card," the voice that went with the hand demanded. Kerry dug in the pocket of her leather jacket and fished out the bit of plastic. "OK." The door was swung open and she was allowed into the small lobby. The woman who admitted her led the way over to the pay desk. She wasn't as hunky as she tried to look, the real muscle was sitting at the back of the office drinking beer and watching a video of last year's Wimbledon.

"Credit," the smallest bouncer stood by the till, waiting to take Kerry's entrance fee. She handed over her card, watched the woman slot it in the register and make the debit. The receipt had 'Leisurecorp Group of Clubs: Social and Gaming' on it. One of her own inventions. Amused, she passed through the lobby and into the bar.

There was a good crowd. Kerry smiled to herself. She liked a crush, the dark, sweaty anonymity of strange bodies sliding against hers in the shove at the bar. All the tables were taken. Women were propped on barstools, leaning against the walls, perched on the back of other women's chairs. The small dance floor was heaving with couples swaying, bathed in purple spotlights. The music was electric, purely synthetic and vaguely funky. Kerry's ear picked out a much-mangled samba rhythm in there somewhere. She made her way to the toilet to check her appearance in the mirror over the washbasin. Vending machines offered dental dams and finger gates in various flavours and strengths. Extra length surgical gloves lubricated with a patent germ-buster were available for those with more dubious habits.

Having re-arranged her hair, she went back to the bar and waited for a drink. She was not in a hurry, looking around her for familiar faces. She took off her jacket and slung it over her shoulder, hooking her thumb through the collar loop. The hide smelt warm against her cheek. She had already spotted three of her ex-lovers and half her housing group. She smiled sweetly at all of them.

Served eventually, she took her drink down to the noisy end of the long narrow room, where the bar lights didn't reach and only the wash of moving colours from the dance floor showed the swaying bodies. She stood watching the dancers, her feet planted firmly apart, back straight and shoulders down.

"Hullo Kerry. How's things?" It was Josie from the Sound Studio. Damn, thought Kerry, friends were all very well, in their place, but she was cruising.

"Fine. How're you? Drowning your sorrows?"

"That's right." Josie eyed her stance, amused. "Am I interrupting something, by any chance?"

"Not yet."

"You live in hope."

"Don't we all." They looked around the crowded room together, the women talking, dancing, watching and being watched.

"Tell me what's happening about our Credit Transfer Facility and I'll let you get back to it."

"It's being dealt with," Kerry said evasively. "I don't think we should talk about it here."

"That's all I wanted to know, really. Not that anyone can hear us, over this crap they're playing. No idea how long, I suppose?" Josie looked hopefully at her.

"You'll be contacted. Not long."

"Thanks. You know we've closed down completely now?"

"I guessed you'd have no choice." Kerry wished she'd go away.

"We kept on as long as we could," Josie settled into a good moan, peering into the bottom of her glass mournfully. "All the equipment's stacked at my house now, in case we lost the premises. Can't bloody move without hacking your shins on an amp. There's congas in the coal shed and guitars everywhere else. Don't know where the zither's got to." Kerry realised that Josie was drunk. "I've got some of the women who used the Studio coming round for lessons still, but it can't go on. Even when I'm only using the practice amp, the neighbourhood watch calls in the filth."

"That's tough. You should live by a motorway, like me. Trombone's nothing to night and day forty tonne lorries."

"Yes, but you don't understand what it's like. . ." Josie took up her tale of woe. Kerry let her drone on, swaying on her feet while she looked around. There were several fascinating women in the room, but all with their less-than-fascinating lovers. A lone woman, on the other side of the bar engaged in the same activity as Kerry, caught her eye and smiled.

"Who's that, do you know?" she interrupted Josie, indicating the stranger.

"Don't bother with her, Kerry, she's got a boyfriend. He's very good, of course, doesn't mind her going with women. . ."

"Oh."

"Bicycles are dangerous."

"I suppose," Kerry turned her back on the woman and searched the other corner of the bar.

"I don't know why you bother," Josie's attention was temporarily diverted. "I gave up cruising years ago."

"It's alright for you," Kerry said, bitterly. "You've got Maz. That's the trouble, everybody else is married."

"You could be," Josie shouted cheerfully.

"No thanks. Anyway, who wants to settle down with a teenager?"

"I'm sure lots of women here think you're very gorgeous," Josie reassured.

"Like who?"

"But it's true if you picked someone up in a bar, it would probably only be a fling. And then you would have all the worry of who they'd been with before, not knowing whether they were reformed substance abusers, or what."

"You sound like a government health warning," Kerry bellowed above the music.

"Well, you've got to think of these things," Josie looked serious.

"What pisses me off is all the women who are old enough to have been around when it didn't matter how many lovers you had."

"What?" Josie cupped her hand to her ear.

"They had all the fun, and now they've settled down monogamously," Kerry continued, ignoring Josie. "And they have the nerve to tell the rest of us it's not safe to do what they did."

"There's a lot of it about," Josie agreed, sagely, having lost the thread of the conversation.

"But I can't help having been born in the eighties," Kerry complained. "I want a good time too."

"Another drink?"

"I'm too young to settle down," Kerry shouted. "I don't like pornographic videos and I can't sublimate my urges by making lots of money, not in my job. What am I supposed to do?"

"Self-abuse?" suggested Josie helpfully.

"Oh, just get me a drink," Kerry sulked.

When Kerry got home, Marlene was pottering about the living room in her nightshirt.

"Want a cup of camomile?" she offered.

Kerry accepted with a grunt of thanks and sat down grumpily. "Can't you sleep?" she asked, as an afterthought.

"No." Marlene tucked her feet up under herself and rubbed her ankles. "Too many things to think about."

"It's not like you to worry yourself sleepless."

"There's a lot to worry about."

"The state of the world." Kerry lit a cigarette. "I know. But it's not going to get any better because you sat up all night thinking about it."

"I'm not." Marlene tried an unconvincing yawn.

"You want to leave it to Ruth anyway. That woman is a semi-professional worrier. Where is she, by the way?"

"Out."

"Well, well. Out for the night, eh? Who would have thought it?"

"I don't think it's like that." Marlene sounded impatient. "She was working late on something at Addie's."

"How disappointing. I thought our saintly sister had finally cracked."

"I wish you two could get on a bit better."

"She disapproves of me."

"You'd be disappointed if she didn't, considering you spend half your time trying to shock her."

"How can I resist?" Kerry appealed. "She gets in such a state. Of course she brings out the wickedness in me. Doesn't she make you want to be outrageous, just for the hell of it?"

"No," Marlene said, bluntly. "That's not my idea of a good time."

"I suppose you think I should grow up," Kerry said, bitterly. "That's Ruth's favourite admonition."

"I didn't say that."

"I don't know how you can get on with Ruth. She's so grim, and you used to be a good time girl."

"Still am." Marlene pulled her dressing gown around her shoulders. "You know I think the most revolutionary thing we can do is to make each other happy."

"So how come you're pacing around at 2 am?"

"My brain was too busy to relax. It's OK, means I get to see you anyway."

"You should have come out with me tonight. That might have helped you to relax."

"Wouldn't I have cramped your style?" Marlene raised her eyebrows.

"Much difference it would have made," Kerry replied, sourly. "I might as well have had a roomful of maiden aunts."

"Poor Kerry," Marlene tried not to laugh. "Were they resisting your fatal charms?"

"Again."

"Admit it, you're quite relieved."

"Not at all."

"What, you mean you actually like all that bother? Going home with a woman you hardly know? All that awkwardness and wasted effort, when you probably won't even see her again?"

"It's better than going home alone."

"You're not alone, sweetness. You've got me, sitting up, nursing my bunions and just thrilled to see you."

"Oh yeah?" Kerry grinned, reluctantly.

"Which would you rather, be honest," Marlene demanded. "A cosy chat with a cosy old friend, or a night of doubtful passion with a stranger? All knees and elbows and uncertainty. And health risks."

"Passion is nice though."

"Cosy old friends are best for that too," Marlene said, firmly.

"Are you suggesting something?"

"Certainly not. Your attempts to be a dangerous dyke have made you distinctly narrow-minded."

"You used to be one yourself," Kerry sulked.

"Don't be cross, dear. You know I love you really. But we all want different things at different times in our lives."

"Meaning?"

"A cruise round the bars isn't my idea of a good time anymore. Sex is never the best the first time, so what's the point of only doing it once and running away? And safe sex with a stranger is too tiresome for words. Even avocado flavoured latex makes me gag."

"Oh god, I suppose you've met a good woman?"

"I meet lots of them," Marlene interrupted.

"And the next thing is you'll be getting married and settling down and none of your friends will ever see you again."

"Hardly likely. Anyway, I haven't done it yet. I just don't regard the idea as quite so horrifying as I used to. Perhaps I'm ready to settle down for a bit. I'd like to be loved for more than twelve hours at a time."

"I wouldn't mind," Kerry complained. "It wouldn't

be so bad if you would just go off and be a super-glue twosome with the woman of your dreams. But you're bound to start trying to convert everyone else to happy coupledom. They always do."

"I don't mind if you want to go on playing the wild rover."

"That's good of you."

"But it isn't making you noticeably happy."

"You see?" Kerry pounced. "Trying to convert me already."

"Your friends are entitled to make these observations. I see you mooching about, trying to look like a real tough, keeping everyone at arm's length in case they find out what a softie you are."

"You know I'm a softie," Kerry pointed out.

"It's taken some time to find out. You're like a hedgehog."

"A spiny exterior is very useful sometimes."

"But does it make you happy?"

"Back to the 'you need a good woman' theory."

"You need something. And you don't seem able to pick it up in a bar."

"Maybe I should keep looking?"

"Maybe," Marlene suggested. "You should admit it's frightening to let someone get close to you."

"I'm close to you, what are you complaining about?" Kerry was aggrieved. "You make me sound like a polar bear."

"You wish." Marlene laughed. "You only trust me as much as you do because you know there's no danger that we'd ever be lovers."

"Especially not if you're going to snuggle down with a monogamous soul-mate. Who is she, by the way?" Kerry waited bitterly to be told 'Ruth', but Marlene dodged the question.

"I don't know if it is going to be like that. It's only at the beginning. I know I feel differently now than I have done in other relationships. I want a bit of commitment. Even some security would be nice."

"Marlene!" Kerry was shocked. "I never thought I'd hear you say that."

"Well," the big woman blushed defensively. "It is

possible that you'll meet someone you care about as much as you care about yourself. And very uncomfortable it is too, I can warn you."

"I wish you the joy of it." Kerry stood up. "Doesn't sound like much fun to me. I'm going to bed, before you start showing me the engagement ring." Marlene stuck out her tongue. "Tell me, which of you gets to have the hen night?" Kerry dodged the cushion which Marlene flung at her, and went upstairs.

* * *

Donna's next-door neighbour Anji sat clutching a handkerchief against her jaw. Donna had filled the cloth square with salt, sewed it up and baked it in the oven until it was almost too hot to touch.

It was past midnight, but Anji couldn't sleep with her toothache and Donna's night-shift body was telling her it was wide-awake time.

"Did you get an appointment with the dentist?"

"Next week," Anji nodded. "Don't know how I'm going to bear it."

"You do look rough," Donna remarked. Anji's eyes were puffy and bloodshot with tiredness. She'd stopped dyeing her hair recently and the silver threads were noticeable now.

"You're too kind," Anji murmured.

"No, really. How are you going to work tomorrow?"

Anji shrugged. "I'll manage. Do I look so bad?"

"Pretty ropey."

"How's Alison?"

"Getting worse."

"Deafer?"

"Yes. She'll never admit she didn't catch something you said, but half the time I think she's lip-reading now. And she's been getting in fights."

"Bet she won."

Donna smiled reluctantly. "I wouldn't like to see the other side. But she doesn't tell me anything."

"Mine are the same."

"But they're boys," Donna protested. "I know that doesn't excuse it, but somehow you expect it more with them."

"Maybe she was being picked on. Kids don't like what's different, you know."

"Even if she was being teased, that's no reason to resort to violence. It's taking the easy way out. It makes you as bad as them."

"Tell Alison all this, not me."

"She knows what I think," Donna compressed her lips disapprovingly. "I only wish they'd get on with her operation."

"No way to hurry it up?"

"We jumped about fifty seven queues already. There's no more fixing to be done, she just has to wait now."

"That's hard on you," Anji picked at a cracked fingernail.

"Harder on her."

"What are they going to do?"

"The operation?"

"Uh huh."

"Put grommets through her ear drums. So the fluid can drain off from her middle ear. It's all blocked up at the moment. That's what makes it hurt. And why she gets all those infections."

"Grommets? Sounds like she should be having it done down the garage, not at hospital."

"They're like little tubes, I think. So all the muck can get out."

"I hope she can stand the waiting."

"I don't know about her," Donna smiled grimly, "I hope I can stand it. She gets so frustrated."

"She's alright, though," Anji sighed. "I wish the ones I have to look after were as nice as her. Most of them are monsters. Maybe their mothers love them, but I can't."

"The ones whose kids don't have any problems probably get places with the registered child-minders."

"And we get what's left over. I wouldn't mind that half of them get brought to me without any breakfast and not potty trained or anything, but it's the parents that take most of the work. Getting them to understand that they can't pay me the regular way, so they have to bring stuff I need from the shops instead."

"Would have thought it'd be simple enough. Don't you give them a list or something?"

"Simple? Don't you believe it." Anji clamped the warm salt pad to her face for comfort. "This woman I take in two little boys for, she brings me fifteen Europounds worth of cake mix last week. Now what am I going to do with that? I give them a list, all nice and clear, but they always think they can bring any old stuff, so long as it adds up to about the right cost. You wouldn't think people could be so stupid."

"Oh no?"

"Maybe you would," she smiled, lopsidedly. "I'm not feeling so kindly today."

"Not surprising." They fell into a comfortable silence for a while. Anji turned her chair sideways to the table and put her feet up on a stool.

"Etty's getting evicted."

"No?" Donna mumbled awake, she'd started to feel drowsy.

"Next week."

"That's short notice."

"I only heard today. We'll have to do something for her."

"Yes. I'll have a word, later this morning. Did you get her Social Credit number?"

Anji reached for her bag and rummaged for a bit of paper, which she handed to Donna.

"There. It shouldn't be too difficult. Hers is condemned and they're not rehousing because she hasn't got the rating for it."

"No trouble."

"I'll tell her." Anji snapped her bag shut and hung it over the back of the chair.

"Better not. She's a bit chatty, isn't she? Nothing against her, but she does talk?"

"C'mon Donna, be fair. The woman's frantic."

"I still think it's best not to tell her," Donna was stubborn. "I'll see if something can be done for her today. Then she'll hear about her rehousing before they evict her. A couple more days won't kill her."

Anji grunted her disagreement, but let it go. Not long afterwards, she buttoned her cardigan firmly and reached for her coat.

"You going?"

"I might get some sleep now. We'll see."

"Take care." Donna got up to show her friend out. "And don't worry about Etty. It won't be long."

"Sure," Anji shrugged, pecked Donna on the cheek and let herself out.

Al joined the mid-day stream of people crowding out of school. Most of the kids headed for the giant burger bar, which could process a thousand customers in half an hour. Those with no money for dinner hung around until they were allowed back into the classrooms.

Security guards hustled the crowd along keeping them on the move. Every shop had someone at the door to prevent more than two pupils coming in at a time. They were seen as a swarm of locusts by the neighbourhood, but locusts who could be made to pay.

Slipping away from the throng, Al walked to the main road and flagged down a minibus. She negotiated a trip to the West End and haggled stubbornly over the price. The driver, who had thought she would be a soft touch, gave way in the end. The impatience of the other passengers subsided. Triumphantly, Al took her seat.

The small video screen at the front of the bus ran a series of adverts with jangling musical tags. A police announcement on wanted persons followed, their pictures flashing across the screen one after another. Missing children, murder victims, identikit abductors and the endless procession of terrorists. On milk cartons and match boxes, on billboards and in commercial breaks, there was no getting away from it. She stared out of the window as they chugged along the bottom of a canyon made by two rows of high-rise office blocks. Half of them stood empty with their workers all put out to free-lance in the home-office network.

In Piccadilly, she signalled the driver to stop and hopped out, dodging the other traffic. With an afternoon of stolen freedom ahead, and credits on her plastic, Al was prepared to enjoy herself. She hummed tunelessly. The credits were stolen too, of course, carefully transferred in the ten minutes of computer down-time when there was no direct link between the machine and her account. Sometimes she found the right time-slot, but it was a risky business.

Brandishing her newly charged card, Al bought a one-day leisure pass and moved through the auto-gates into the Techno Theme park. It had once been a real park, Green Park. There were still trees, around the edges. They didn't interfere with the exhibition domes, silver grey blobs of interlocking hexagonal panels. The trees were scaly-barked diseased things, soon to die despite the preservation orders lavished upon them. The "rainforest experience" exhibit was more appealing anyway.

Al pursued her enjoyments thoroughly. The chamber of holograms didn't frighten her, either she was getting too old, or it needed the sound effects to convince. The laser-battle display thrilled her, the speed and colours. Even the depressed man giving out leaflets at the entrance couldn't put her off. So what if the show was the only successful result of a multi-billion dollar space war research programme? Al wasn't a taxpayer. She slouched off, crumpling the leaflet, and had synthetic raw fish in the Japanese dome.

No-one took any notice of her, although the public were constantly warned that children alone were at risk, and should be reported. She was comfortably scruffy, in her oldest clothes. That morning, Donna had screamed at her, like she did once every so often, to wear a dress. Why did she bother? Al couldn't understand. She never did end up wearing the dress. Sometimes Donna would go on at her for hours, but she could never be sure whether Al was making the effort to listen, so she usually gave up. It didn't used to bug her so much, she made jokes about tom-boys. Lately she had got more of a thing about it. Al sighed, and bought herself some cigarettes.

At dusk, she staggered out of the anti-matter ride

feeling squashed and dizzy. The park was lit up in bright, flashing colours. Hundreds of people milled around, their faces glowing purple in the artificial light. Everybody else was there with someone. They had some reason to laugh and scream and grab each other's hands on the scary rides. Al enjoyed her independence, but she knew the park wasn't made for loners. She pushed her way through the crowd.

Away from the noise and lights of the expo-domes, beyond the palings and autogates, there was a small patch of sorry looking trees and grass. It was the only part of the park which you didn't have to pay to get into. A man lay on his back beneath a tree. Tucked under his arm, clinging to him, with her face buried against his shoulder, was a woman. He watched the baseball game on his wrist video. Al hurried past them, faintly disgusted.

There was an old bench, with no slats. She perched on its metal frame and lit a cigarette. Donna might smell it on her breath when she got home, but she wasn't in a hurry to go back there. She had spent her entire life in a three room flat with her mother, it was beginning to feel more like a 'Correction in the Community' program than a happy home. Donna kept a picture of the vicarage in Milwall where Al had been conceived, but her father had been beaten to death at a bus stop by football fans before Al had made her first appearance.

There was a tramp scavenging in the rubbish bins. Man or woman, Al couldn't tell. It looked like a bale of cloth scraps at the recyclers, tied up with string. Or one of those bundles of cast-offs that American charities sent over for the deserving destitute. The girl hummed tunelessly and watched the tramp hurling things out of the bin like a dog at a rat-hole. Some of the objects were seized and stowed away in pockets or bags, but it was hard to see what made them more precious than the rest of the rubbish.

Another derelict, with a thin grey beard, shuffled up. He peered sadly at the heap of discarded scraps and cartons at the feet of the first rummager, as though deploring the mess. He stooped to pick over the leavings, while trying to look as though he was just having a bit of a tidy up. The bundle of jumpers and coats snarled at him territorially, seeing him off.

The senior vagrant finished rifling the garbage and stomped towards the bench with her haul. It was a woman, Al realised, seeing her face for the first time. She spread a collapsed cardboard crate across the struts of the ruined bench and sat down heavily. She smelt appalling. Al wrinkled her nose.

"Bloody horrible noise," the tramp said, abruptly. "Can't you carry a tune, or what?" She mumbled her words, Al didn't hear. The tramp shot out a strong, knobbly forefinger and poked her in the arm. "I said, do you call that singing?"

"Don't call it anything." Al rubbed her arm and stared at the woman.

"Deaf?"

"Yeah."

The woman nodded and muttered to herself. It was hard to tell how old she was. Anywhere between thirty and seventy, Al thought.

"Don't mumble like that, it's not fair. You talking to me or not?" she protested.

"Not, definitely not. I've got out of the habit. Talking to myself, but you can't hear and I can't help it."

"How old are you?" Al peered into the woman's face to follow her lips moving, should she answer.

"I forgot. You're going to ask me what's my name, aren't you? Don't bother, I forgot that too. You're better off without. Me, I don't exist, officially."

"No?"

"Better that way," she pulled a paisley dressing gown from one of her bags and put it on for another layer of warmth. "They pick me up, for vagrancy. Then they let me out, and I don't exist anymore. They don't know to come looking for me. Not on their records, you see."

"Do you get picked up a lot?"

"I just got out. They made me leave the pram." She scowled. Al decided she was mad and started edging away.

"That's tough."

"All my things. I couldn't carry them, so I had a pram. Everything I had. It was home." She smacked her fist against her thigh. "Only to them, it looked like a heap of junk. My things. You think 'she's a drunk'. It's appearances."

"No I don't."

"Suppose you aren't afraid of me either?"

"No."

"Liar. Everyone's afraid of everybody else."

"Why should I be afraid of you?" Al glanced speculatively at the woman, "Not dangerous, are you?"

"'Course I'm dangerous," she leered menacingly. "Poor and mad, aren't I? A failure. It might be contagious. Deathshead at the wedding feast."

"Are you mad?" Al stayed, curiosity overcoming fear. "Really?"

"Talk to myself, don't I?" The woman smiled, slyly. "Choose to live like this. Must be mad."

"I didn't know you chose."

"Once I did. There were other possibilities."

"So why d'you want to be a baggie?" Al stared at her rudely.

"Because I'd rather be a free nobody than a comfortable statistic. You know what freedom is?"

Al shrugged. Maybe the tramp was mad, after all. Of all the stupid questions.

"How old are you?"

"Fourteen."

"You look pregnant." A dirty finger shot out and poked Al's chest.

"It's the MammalianMetaTropine in the milk," explained Al. "They give it to the cows for the milk yield. All the kids have swollen breasts, even the boys."

"You can give me one of those," without waiting for permission the woman snatched a cigarette. Al carelessly tossed the pack into her lap.

"Keep them."

The woman squinted at her suspiciously. "How come a tyke like you has the money for this sort of thing?"

"I've got money," Al sighed. "As much as you like. And fuck all to spend it on."

"Doesn't sound like too much of a problem to me," the woman snorted.

"You should know. How it is with ID and that. They've got you there." She pressed her thumb down on the bare frame of the bench on which she perched.

"Spending is all you think about. Kids. Consumercraft in schools, you're all alike. Did you steal it?"

Al smiled and said nothing. The tramp grunted.

"So why can't you spend it?"

"I can't buy things, you know, like objects. I couldn't take them home, 'cos my mum's so stuck on the straight and narrow, it's silly. I can sneak the odd peripheral for the pc, only because she's too dull to know what they cost. But nothing large, or findable, or she just goes on and on forever. She goes through my stuff, you know. Doesn't trust me."

"Poor kid. Cut off from consumer durables." The tramp curled her lip.

"It's alright for you," Al was indignant. "You chose to be a tramp. I don't want to be poor. It's stupid."

"So what do you do with your unspendable credit?"

"Things like that," Al jerked her thumb in the direction of the brightly lit domes and rides. "Going out. Kids' stuff. It's nice enough when you've bunked off school. But I've still got to worry in case a truant patrol pulls me up for an ID check."

"Big deal. I used to work Oxford Circus 'Spare us something for a cup of tea'. But you can't throw credit into a beggar's hand. I miss coins, you know. They were real. Never had much of the paper stuff. Sometimes I forget they stopped all that."

"I don't care how it comes, so long as I can spend it."

"You are like all the other kids. Greedy. What do you want to do that you can't?"

Al hugged her knees to her chest and shifted on her perch. "Just go somewhere, find a place where there's no drug tests and blood tests and lie-detectors and ID checks. Just get on a flight to some place with no visas or sponsors or vetting. Somewhere they don't have Social Credit ratings or rat-eaten tower blocks. A nice hot country where I didn't have to spend half the sodding winter laid up with earache."

"Not asking much, eh?"

"Bloody ridiculous, isn't it?" Al cleared her throat and spat. "I can't even take a day trip out of town, without the booking clerk reporting to the police, since they started checking with your school and parents that you weren't absconding. I can't go into a pub, 'cos I haven't got over-eighteen ID. I can only steal piddling little amounts of money."

"Why?"

"Jesus, where have you been for the last few years?"

"Around and about," the woman smiled. "I've not had a lot to do with Banking Societies though."

"I bet. Your account, well, not yours if you haven't got one, but everybody else has. Anyway, the account's linked to your Social Credit rating, and if there's 'inappropriate levels of activity' they report it to the tax people. Who shop you to the police."

"So the poor stay poor? That's our lot."

"Something like that. Smart people must have about five different IDs and offshore banking, all that. It takes money to set up."

"You're smart, aren't you?" The woman had a twisted smile. Al didn't feel that she was being praised. "You're not afraid of computers, are you? Oh, no. You don't want to change anything do you? Just fiddle it a bit here and there. So how come you're still stuck at the bottom of the heap? Poorish and powerless? How come you didn't programme yourself out of that yet?"

"You're scared of machines, so you think we all should be, is that it?"

"Selfish kids like you. Always fighting your way out and devil take the hindmost. That's why nothing changes. When you're rich, you'll need the poor. Otherwise, you wouldn't know you were better off. I'll be doing you a favour, being a tramp."

"You don't know," Al scowled. "You don't know what I do, or who I help."

"And you're not going to tell me, in case I'm Security in disguise."

"You could be," Al sulked. "I don't even know your name."

"Who wants to? Anyway, I told you, I forgot it. You didn't answer my question. Why haven't you moved on to better things yet?"

"It's my mum." Al stuck her fists in her pockets, the night was getting cool. "She's got this thing about honesty. It's stupid. She goes out to work, really crummy jobs. Knackers herself. And I could make the same money in ten minutes at the computer. She won't have it though. And I sort of owe her. I mean, part of the reason she does all the work is to keep me, right? So long as I live with her, I guess I have to go along with how she wants to do things. More or less."

"You could leave. Have all the things you want. Get shot of her morals. I thought selfish was your middle name. Forget her."

"Oh yeah," Al sneered. "Really likely. It's so easy, when you're my age, to walk away from all that. Don't you know how many laws there are against kids going off by themselves? You're always being checked up on, hassled and bloody cared for. Parent power, don't you remember?"

"Talk big, scared to act," the tramp taunted.

"Oh sod off."

The woman made some quiet dismissive remark, her face half turned away. Al jumped to her feet and stood in front of the woman screaming at her.

"Don't you do that. Don't you fucking hide what you're saying from me. It's easy, having an argument with someone who's deaf, isn't it? You can always get the last word. Stinking old bag. Dirty tramp. Who do you think you are, anyway?" She stood there, shaking with rage.

"I'm sorry," the woman said loudly.

"And you don't have to shout, either. What's got into you? You were talking fine before."

"I'm sorry," she said again, more normally. "Maybe

I am a bit mad, you know. I lose my temper sometimes. I wish that things weren't the way that they are. I shouldn't take it out on you."

"No you shouldn't. Look, I've got to be going. It's late."

"Do something for me?"

"What?" Al looked suspiciously at the woman.

"You've got money, and nothing to spend it on. I haven't eaten all day. Buy me some food."

"You've got a cheek." Al considered. "Yeah, OK. Though I don't suppose they'd let us in anywhere. I'll get you a carry out."

The woman stood up stiffly, her hips clunking noisily back into their sockets. Carefully not muttering to herself, she followed Al out of the park.

Kerry was disgusted with her bicycle. She kicked its little solid wheels, with their slippery acetate tyres and dragged it off the road onto the pavement by the long, banana-shaped handle bars. She would have to start saving up for a car, she decided, anything but this heap of tele-order junk, which kept packing up.

She should have come home last night, after the rehearsal, only she was too smashed to ride back. And of course, by the morning the batteries had had time to leak themselves flat, so she was going to be late for work, plus she felt gritty and uncomfortable from having slept on the floor in a strange sleeping bag that smelt of other people's feet, while the heavy and breathless pet dog of the house lay on her legs and went to sleep. So had her legs, eventually.

Over her shoulder was slung her trombone in the hard black shell of its case. She knew she looked like Davey Crockett going to shoot moose, but it was the easiest way to carry it. She trudged the last half mile home against the morning traffic jam of four lanes of cars coming into London from the western suburbs and the Berkshire commuter belt. One man, one car, she thought disgustedly watching the businessmen in their shirt sleeves and company perks, chatting to each other on their car phones. Like some divine political right. They could go and sit in their cars in the drive at home and make all their calls without moving a metre. Then at the end of the day, they could get out, trot up the garden path shouting "I'm home" and the lady wife could coo from the kitchen "Have a good day in the car, dear?".

The air was visibly thickening beside the A4(M). Kerry could feel the crud from a thousand idling engines find its way between her eyelids and contact lenses. They scoured each other every time she blinked.

A few hundred yards up the road from her house she stopped. There were at least five police cars pulled up on the pavement ahead. Round the corner, she could see the tail of a van. A team of dog handlers was searching around the boarded up basements. One policeman stood at the bottom of the steps to her own house leaning casually on the handle of an axe, and she saw that her front door had been smashed in. Three of the women from the next house along were being bundled down the steps in handcuffs, obviously hauled straight out of bed. None of them was wearing socks or coats. Kerry made a mental note of their names as they were pushed into a large van with bars across the windows and no door handles on the inside.

She leant her bike against a wall and ambled up, hands in pockets, to join the small crowd of passers-by who had stopped to watch, hoping her face didn't give her away. There were at least fifty police in sight, wearing their flame-proof overalls, face masks and black vinyl, virus-proof gloves. She strolled up to the corner and peered into the vans which had brought them. Five of them, almost blocking the side street, and the dog vans. She saw the riot shields and crash helmets piled in the vans and wondered why they had thought all this necessary for a few houses full of sleeping women. She turned a corner onto the path that led behind the houses. She could see her own garden, full of blue uniforms, two of them standing on the flat roof of the living room, one of them in the garden yelling through the window with a loud hailer. So, Marlene and Ruth had barricaded themselves in. They'd be wiping the disks of anything incriminating. It should only take a few minutes.

Kerry was holding her breath, her lower lip clamped firmly between her teeth. Go on, she thought fiercely. The police at the window wouldn't be able to see whoever was sitting at the computer. Ruth, probably. That sounded like Marlene, yelling against the loud hailer, distracting them for the time it took to get rid of all the work they were doing on Credit Transfer Facilities for women's groups. She could hear the regular thuds of an axe on wood from inside the house. They were knocking the door in. Not long now. Ahead of her a flat hat called out "My men, to me" and a patrol of policemen swarmed over the garden walls to join their inspector on the path.

"Around to the front, at the double," he shouted crisply. The patrol formed into two lines and began running along the narrow path, towards Kerry and the side street. She squeezed herself against the fence that led onto the railway line and watched the dozen men running heavily, their boots hitting concrete in rough time. She could see the truncheons in their trouser pockets striking against their legs. As they passed her, she was bumped and shoved against the rusty chain link fence. One of the men caught her a backward blow with his elbow, not even looking round to see what she would make of it.

They would be bringing Marlene and Ruth out the front of the house. She started to run back the way she had come, then forced herself to slow to a walk, stuck her hands in her pockets and whistled. The tune was "Stormy Weather" she noted automatically.

The crowd was larger now at the front of the house. Two policewomen had been detailed to keep the onlookers in their place. They stood waving their arms as the neighbourhood pushed forward, growling "Get back" as gruffly as they could manage, making palms out pushing gestures. Kerry joined in, one row back from the first of the little group of rubberneckers, looking wide-eyed.

Five women from next door the other side were being bundled into vans. Poor sods. They'd been driving all night to get home from their walking holiday. Kath was hauled out in a thermal undershirt and fibre pile jacket, wearing a dazed expression and her hiking boots. She opened her mouth when she saw Kerry, but got the message of the blank stare and the slight shake of the head and shut it again.

There was a hitch. The police had run out of

prisoner-proof vans. They kept their latest catch standing on the pavement handcuffed together. Five women stood looking bemused, sullen, angry or bored. Kerry didn't suppose it was the first time for any of them.

The splintered remains of her own front door were kicked aside. Marlene and Ruth were being brought out. Kerry could hear Marlene already, a non-stop torrent of abuse at full-volume. The policewoman to whom she was handcuffed was dragged along in the wake of six foot solid of stroppy captive. "Come along now" she kept saying, pointlessly. "That's enough of that." Her male colleagues stood back and grinned unpleasantly, until one of them caught the rough side of Marlene's tongue. Not liking it, he stepped up to where she stood on the pavement and cracked his truncheon across her short-ribs, knocking the breath out of her. She swayed dizzily against Ruth, gasping for air.

Ruth had seen Kerry. She let her gaze slide casually over the crowd. She met Kerry's eyes for a second and smiled faintly. Kerry raised an eyebrow and Ruth nodded. Then she turned her attention back to Marlene, who was recovering but subdued. Kerry knew Ruth was trying to reassure her, so she guessed they'd had time to wipe the disks. A lot of work down the drain, but it was safer. The pass words and codes wouldn't have held out for long. Pass words and codes were too easy to crack, that's what had made their whole operation possible in the first place. But it cut both ways.

A rush of sirens headed towards them and another two vans with barred windows and the metropolitan police crest tastefully picked out on the door crammed their way onto the pavement. The remaining women were loaded up, Kerry didn't wait to see in which direction they would head, but set off back down the road to the tube station. Time to call a lawyer.

There was a bank of phones at the station. One of them had been vandalised, two were flashing up "999 calls only" signs and there was a queue for the one which worked. Kerry thought of ringing the police and announcing that her house had been broken into, but decided against it. This was no time to confront the repressive state apparatus with the weapon of irony.

The woman ahead of her in the queue was calling the Social to complain about her benefit. It was a long call. Kerry tried not to fidget as the woman got transferred from department to department and put on hold in each. The digits flashed up alarmingly in the charge box. She appeared to get through, finally, about two seconds before the credits on her phone card expired and she was cut off. She slammed the phone down and crashed into Kerry, staring at her with tears of rage and frustration in her eyes.

"Where do they sell fucking phone cards round here?" she hissed furiously. Kerry jerked her thumb in the direction of the newsagent's kiosk and stepped up to take her turn, feeling heartless. She could hear the paper seller start to deliver his usual little chat about not letting things get to you while she dialled the solicitors' number which Ruth had made her learn, in case of emergency.

It rang engaged. She waited a minute and dialled again. Ignoring the mutters of the queue behind her, she tried a third time. The practice had quite a large switchboard, she knew, at least six lines. Still engaged. That meant incoming calls to them were being blocked. She swore. Of course their solicitor was well known for doing women's cases, they would jam her phone if they were rounding up the local branch of the lesbian ghetto. She'd have to go round there. The man behind her tapped her on the shoulder.

"Are you going to be all day?" The people behind him nodded approvingly.

"Fuck off, you wanker, or I'll break your face in half." He took a step backwards, looking surprised.

"Well!"

Not waiting to find out what he thought of her manners she quickly dialled another number. She got through to the hospital, left a message in her department that she was off sick. As she hustled her way out of the station, she saw the woman who had been calling the Social shuffle grimly to the back of the queue clutching her new phone card.

The solicitor's office was in Camden. She'd take the bike round the corner to the garage and charge the battery. She checked the house in passing. There was a young constable sitting on one of the kitchen chairs in the hall, almost out of sight. Waiting for any residents who had missed the fun she guessed. At least she wouldn't have to worry about burglars, despite the door being off at the hinges.

She walked on, the trombone bumping against the small of her back, listing the things she had to do. Solicitor. They'd probably taken them to Shepherd's Bush Road. She would have to get someone up there to check it out. She had better not go herself. She should try and send a discreet message to the refuge they'd been working for, to let them know that their Credit Transfer Facility wouldn't be fixed up this week after all.

She got to where she'd left the bike and it was gone. She must have forgotten to lock it up. Some bastard had swiped it, under the noses of fifty policemen and the interested gaze of what she felt sure was the entire neighbourhood watch committee. She started running back to the tube station. Maybe it was going to be that sort of a day.

* * *

Marlene leant against the door of her cell, nursing her bruised ribs. The cell was bare, apart from a plastic covered mat on the concrete floor and a toilet with no seat. The tiny panes of thick securiplex kept out most of the daylight. Through the observation panel in the metal door, she could hear the ratchet-like clicking of an asthmatic breathing. Zoe, without her medication, must be next door.

They were in a bay of four single cells, leading off a short corridor. She knew Ruth was opposite, but there was little to see outside. The red eye of the thermal image finder blinked as it scanned the empty corridor.

Out of reach, in the corner of her own cell, a camera stared down at her. The blanket on the sleeping mat was filthy, but the cell, though stuffy, felt cold and draughty. Marlene shivered, she was suffering from shock, and wrapped the disgusting fabric around her shoulders.

In her brick box, Ruth tried to count the hours since their arrest. Her watch had been taken when she was strip-searched. There had been an unpleasant knowingness about the policewoman who had explored her in surgical gloves. Ruth speculated as to whether her recreations differed much from her work.

There had been twelve of them seized altogether. Ruth wondered what the others would say. In her initial panic, she had seen that most of the Credit Transfer group was present and concluded that they must have been targeted. But then she had been cautioned on a charge of conspiracy to defraud the Department of Social Security. That had puzzled her – whatever the others might be doing in that respect, she was not involved. As possibly the only one who could afford a lawyer, she had repeatedly asked to see the duty solicitor. The officer who had been processing her at the time had laughed and entered her name as 'helping with enquiries'. Even if they were sticking to the rules, they could hold her for seventy two hours without telling anybody.

* * *

Letchley might have been designed by a statistician. He had lost an average number of teeth to the commonest sort of gum disease. His height, build and outlook were medium. He was loyal to his firm, ambitious, but not dynamic. An actuary would insure him for three score year and ten without hesitation. He had never voted for any of the New Right parties, finding extremism disagreeable. His wife, when leaving him, had said "It's nothing personal, Jason," and indeed, by that time he could hardly remember why they had married. At least they had never fought.

Throughout a long and tedious day in the bowels

of Shepherd's Bush Road police station, Letchley continued unruffled and interested. Although he had caught many criminals, through meticulous checking of their account records, he had never before been involved in direct confrontations with suspects. He found police routine mildly exciting.

Higgin was less sanguin. As the day wore into evening, he could hardly console himself with the thought of his block overtime. One after another, the women were brought down to the interview room. Letchley might regard them as fascinating creatures from another world, but to Higgin they were an everyday matter. Each was threatened with prosecution – for petty things to do with benefits or foodstamps or failing to register for tax. It was useful, thought Higgin, how many laws there were for the dregs to break. Poverty was criminal. Having been menaced, the women were invited to tell about the groups with which they were involved, that had false Credit Transfer Facilities. Even with the lure of immunity on their other crimes, none had accepted the invitation.

Between them, Higgin and Letchley had threatened or frightened, been brisk, bored or fatherly with all of the women. None had responded. Higgin was fed up. His tongue had a metallic coating from too much coffee and tobacco, he didn't even have an office to call his own. He hated working in strange stations, with strange canteens, perched in a borrowed interview room and having to ask favours of the desk sergeant.

Higgin and Letchley sat on uncomfortable metal and plastic chairs in the depressing interview room, waiting for the next woman to be brought along from the cells. A bored and burly uniformed officer, there to take notes, tipped his chair against the wall and blew smoke rings carefully through each other.

"We're not getting much joy, are we?" Higgin complained. He was beginning to think the whole thing was a waste of time.

"We've caught out some benefit frauds."

"Small stuff. That's not what you're here for,

anyway." Marlene was being led into the room, looking sore and angry.

"Sit down." Higgin pointed to a chair on the other side of the small metal table. The note-taker, uninterested, settled himself once more to his task. He switched on the audio-video recorder, tapping the built-in mike with a gesture equivalent to licking the end of his pencil and starting a new page. Higgin rubbed his big red hands together. The woman opposite him said nothing, staring with unlimited hostility.

"You've been a bit naughty, haven't you," he began, unbothered by her tough pose. Letchley, at his side, sat with his arms folded and a stern magisterial frown.

"Tell me about it," Marlene said, sitting straight and expansive. Her legs took up most of the space under the table, as this ham-faced man would find out if he moved.

"I don't really need to tell you about it do I? You claim Income Assistance."

"So? I'm unemployed. I'm entitled."

"But only for six months. After that you're not entitled to anything."

"I haven't been signing on six months yet."

"What was your job, before?"

"I was travelling. Abroad."

"We can check whether your passport number was logged in or out of the country, you know."

"There was an immigration officers' strike when I came back. So there won't be any record."

"How very convenient," Higgin sneered. Letchley watched his interview technique with an air of detached interest. Obviously his colleage was trying to be subtle with this one. It threw a new light on him.

"Not at all. We were stuck at Heathrow for two days because of it."

"What about Mary Jones?" Higgin snapped suddenly. He lit a cigarette for effect and blew smoke in Marlene's face.

"Who she?" Marlene looked aggressive but inside she felt the stomach-turning greyness of fear.

"I suppose you've never heard of Barbara MacIntosh or Wilma Spedding either?"

"Nope."

"Despite the fact that they all lived in the same house as you?"

"There's a lot of to-ing and fro-ing there. And I only moved in a few months ago myself."

"Would it interest you to hear that all these women claimed Income Assistance for the six months it's available, from your address, and then vanished?"

"Goodness." Marlene picked up the packet of cigarettes which Higgin had left on the table, took one, lit it and blew smoke back at him.

"Or to hear that all these women died when they were children? That their birth certificates were used to get false Social Credit numbers?"

"Fancy that." Marlene shook her head wonderingly, but she was trying desperately to work out how much they knew, and how much she could bluff.

"I'm sure if we dug a bit into your current identity, we'd find that Gillian Prebble was laid to rest in some small town cemetery, twenty odd years ago."

"You think so?"

"I'm certain of it. So you see, there's no point being evasive with us. We've got you coming and going." Higgin ticked off points on his round sweaty fingers. "Fraud on the benefits. Impersonation. Making a false statement for the purposes of obtaining a Social Credit number. Giving a false name to the police. Giving false information to the Registrar of Births and Deaths." Higgin ran out of fingers and stopped. "That should do to be going on with, don't you think?"

She glared at him. "I'm not saying anything. I haven't done anything wrong."

"You're not saying anything because you've got some listening to do." Higgin leaned forward and thrust his face very close to her.

"Since there's no chance I'd ever sit and listen to you if we weren't locked in a room together, you'd better make the most of it." She was beginning to wonder about the pudgy copper's silent sidekick.

"I am prepared to consider offering you a way out."

Higgin was still very close, she could feel his breath on her face, see the join where the economy crowns on his teeth didn't match the original enamel.

Her scalp contracted. "What do you want?"

He looked her up and down, but given the way she was looming over him, mostly up. "I'm not convinced you're a deserving case for my good efforts. I might just leave you to rot in the cells until they can get you to court."

"Why don't you tell me what you want?" She was frightened, but also intrigued. Higgin knew he had her nearly hooked, and glanced at Letchley, to make sure the man from the Banking Societies was paying attention to his methods.

"Just a little co-operation," he spread his hands and shrugged. "A chat about this and that, and who knows? We might even manage to lose your file. It can be done."

"A chat about what?"

"Ah."

"It's no good expecting me to guess what you're on about."

Letchley suddenly cleared his throat. It was a small, precise sound, and everyone in the room turned to look at him. He had been busy with his lap-top computer, and now looked up, to a point in the air between Higgin and Marlene.

"You are a member of the management committee of a refuge for battered wives," he produced the phrase carefully, "in Acton," he said.

"I was," Marlene corrected. "Before it was closed down."

"It is my belief that it never did close down. After the Refuge was refused a Credit Transfer Facility, it began doing business in the guise of Home Security Consultants. The balance of the Refuge funds were taken out of the country and probably rechannelled to Home Security via Switzerland.

"Probably? You mean you're guessing?" Marlene pounced on the vagueness of Letchley's case, though her heart had sunk when he started talking about the Refuge.

"Swiss banking traditions," he waved them aside with an irritated gesture. "However, there is enough evidence in this country of the link between the Refuge and the Security firm, which sprang phoenix-like to life the month after the Refuge closed, and occupies the same premises." He looked unruffled again.

"So?" Marlene acted belligerent, stalling. She rolled up the sleeves of her heavy workshirt, and dumped her elbows on the table in a way that made it shake on its tubular legs.

"You were on the management committee of the Refuge," Higgin joined in, harder in tone. Goddess preserve me, thought Marlene, they're trying to play hard cop/soft cop. How quaint. "And you've been seen going into the offices of the alleged Home Security Consultants, which is in fact still operating as a place for women to run away from their husbands and hide in. So you must know how the false Credit Transfer set-up was done. And more to the point, who did it."

"We want names," Letchley leered at her. He was fascinated by her size and the great round swell of muscle in her bare forearms as they lay on the table.

"I don't know what you're talking about." Her answers were automatic, she was thinking furiously. They had more guesswork than proof here, that was obvious, but they were uncomfortably close and interested.

"Yes you do." Higgin lit another cigarette and carefully put the packet out of reach. "And we want to know too."

"We want to know who got you the Credit Transfer Facility," Letchley demanded. "And we don't want the middlemen and the messengers. We want the men in charge."

"I don't know nothing." Marlene sat back and folded her arms across her chest, her face a picture of blank stupidity. She was relieved. They didn't know who was doing the Credit arrangements. This was a fishing expedition and they had picked her up because of her involvement with the Refuge. She checked through all the other women who had been arrested with her. They were all in one or another of the groups which had been fixed up with new Credit Transfer Facilities, as well as being members of the Credit Transfer group itself. None of them were about to confess to being part of a major criminal conspiracy in order to get off a minor benefit fraud. Everyone fiddled the Social, it was true, you couldn't live on it. That was more likely to mean a fine than anything. She totted up what they had over her and came up with six months inside as the worst case. She cringed at the thought.

The two men opposite sat watching her in silence. The record-keeper stared into space, bored comatose by the proceedings. Minutes passed, smoke drifted slowly from the cigarette in Higgin's hand to find its way out to the street around the edge of a badly fitting window. It was dark outside and the fluorescent glare in the interview room gave them all depressing shadows under the eyes and chin.

"I don't know what you're on about," Marlene said at length, looking as bland as she could.

"We'll have to give you time to think about the possibilities," Higgin menaced. "You sleep on it. Take her away." The spare constable led her out.

"Bugger that," Higgin said, when she was gone.

"Not very helpful."

"Ignorant slag. Didn't know what we were on about, I reckon."

"You think so?" Letchley stroked his chin, considering. "No, I must disagree there. I think she probably knows somewhat more than she's telling."

"Maybe we didn't lay on the Income Assistance stuff heavy enough. Maybe she's too dense to take in that we could get a custodial on that one."

"I doubt it. You made it fairly plain."

"Well, I tell you, I've had it up to here with this. I don't think any of these bloody women know what time of day it is, let alone who's running the Credit Transfer fraud."

"Some of them must know," Letchley argued.

"They undeniably have connections with organisations that have false Credit Transfer identities. You could start proceedings against them for the various other misdemeanours and see if that shakes them up."

"I don't think we're going to get anything out of them," Higgin repeated gloomily. "We're wasting our time."

"We could try letting them go. Now we've rattled them. See who they run off to tell."

"My god, Letchley, have you got any idea what the Super would say if I asked for a team to do surveillance on all of that shower? He'd go spare. We're cash limited, you know."

"It would be worth it. They are bound to try and get in touch with the people higher up in the organisation. I suppose their phones are tapped?"

"Of course."

"And the mail?"

"Yes," Higgin grunted. "I suppose we could spare a couple of blokes. They all live in the same bloody road, which makes things easier. I know the Super will say you and me have to muck in on this one though. And sitting in a car all day, watching unmoving lace curtains ain't what I'm accustomed to, I can tell you."

"I'm sure the experience will be very interesting. Grass roots police work, as it were. Today has been most informative, by the way." Letchley's eyes gleamed slightly. Higgin looked at him in mild amazement.

"One thing I can tell you about watching people, mate, is that it's not an 'interesting experience'. People are pretty fucking boring. They're like you and me, only drearier."

"But we'll do it?"

"Yes, though I don't hold out much hope. If we can scare anything out of them while they're in here. . ." Higgin rubbed his tired eyes.

"We've got them for the rest of the night, haven't we?"

"Maybe I'll have another go at that prissy one. Ruth whatsername. She was too tight lipped by half. That's the only thing that makes me think you could be right.

They act like they're either dead ignorant or got something to hide."

"Let's hope we'll find out which."

* * *

The clatter of the cell door being unlocked woke Ruth. She struggled up from the pallet on the floor feeling dazed and dirty. The ceiling light had been left on, but she thought it must be the middle of the night.

Higgin stepped into the cell, leaving the door ajar. She thought of pushing past him, but his stocky frame was bulky with muscle and she had no idea of the way out of the station. Backing into the corner, as he advanced towards her, she smelt his sour sweat and her own, similarly pungent. The policeman said nothing, watching her as she tried to work some saliva into her dry mouth. Ruth stood apprehensively, waiting for him to speak.

"Shout for help," he said at last. "Scream. Go on." She was silent. "I said scream, you cunt." He slapped her. Ruth shouted, nothing happened. He waited, smiling, knowing no-one would come.

"Some things I should explain," Higgin began, leaning his hands against the wall, either side of Ruth's head. "You lay a finger on me and it's 'assaulting a police offer in the execution of his duty'." He offered his cheek for a revenge slap, mockingly. She didn't move. "I can splatter you all round the walls of this cell, and if you say anything, they're self-inflicted injuries and you're maliciously making a false complaint."

She swallowed and tried to meet his eye. His gaze was so intrusive, she had to look away. A muscle at the corner of her mouth began to twitch and her legs trembled.

"Why haven't you got a boyfriend?" he asked, pleasantly. "Your friends couldn't get one. Dirty slags. But you could, if you tried. Made yourself nice."

"No, thanks," her voice sounded thin and flat, she wasn't breathing properly.

"My wife doesn't like me when I haven't shaved." He ground his stubbly chin painfully into her neck. She could hear the bristles scraping against skin, trapped in her corner. "But you don't mind, do you?" He stood back and looked at her. "You'd be glad to find out what it's like with a man, wouldn't you?"

"No." She began to feel quite distant from the proceedings.

"Are you a prostitute then?" his voice lifted at the end of his sentences, reminding her, incongruously, of holidays in Suffolk.

"No."

"My friend Letchley says all pros are lezzies. He reads a lot of books. You're one, aren't you?"

"No," she said again.

"Not a les?" he teased. "I don't believe you. Even with all that pretty hair," he pulled a handful of it, forcing her head up to look at him. "Which is your butch then? The big girl with the cracked ribs? You could do better."

"I'm not a prostitute," she said, her throat tight.

"You won't know Carole then. She was a working girl."

"I've never met her."

"Maybe you have. She lived just around the corner from you. We had her in this very cell."

"I don't know anyone called Carole."

"Don't you?" Higgin's eyes, which were very pale and slightly protuberant, rolled at her. "She's dead now. In here one minute, stiffed it the next. Funny how it happens."

Ruth didn't believe him. The feeling that she was floating above the scene, detached, was growing.

"Carole got some business help. Found a woman who could get her a dodgy Credit Transfer Facility. She said it was a dyke. Couldn't have been you, could it?" He fingered the collar of her jacket. "I mean, you don't look like what you are, do you? Maybe it was your girlfriend. No mistaking her, is there?"

"I don't know what you are talking about."

"Maybe your friend's got a sideline. Didn't she tell you? Or maybe it was one of your other mates. You should tell me about it. Educated girl like you, shouldn't be mixed up in all that."

"All what?" There was enough genuine ignorance in her voice to stop him pursuing it. She had never heard of a prostitute called Carole and didn't believe Marlene would have anything to do with such a woman.

"You're not being very friendly," Higgin complained. "Why don't you try being nice to me?"

Ruth squirmed out of his reach, unable to bear his breath upon her face. Higgin caught her roughly by the arm and pulled her back, to remind her of his power, then let her go.

"Don't forget," he said, "you'll be here all night. And you can't get the door unlocked, but I can." Still smiling, as he had throughout, Higgin left the cell.

* * *

Kerry was mending the front door at dawn. It was a bright, crisp morning, full of spring, and despite the anxieties of the last twenty four hours, she whistled cheerfully.

The police had hung around until half-way through the night. Even when she'd seen the end-of-shift van come for the last of them, she'd still waited, perched on the tilting seat of the bus stop opposite, pretending to be a dosser.

She hammered at the broken panels, knocking them out with a small axe. The door was a write-off, she smashed out the fragments and unscrewed it at the hinges. "At least the neighbours won't complain about the noise at this unreasonable hour," she thought, "since all the neighbours are in police custody."

The junk room had a heavy door on it, with a hold for the barrel of a lock. It would have to do as a stand-in. She attacked its hinges, the screws were rusty and hidden under thick coats of ageing gloss paint. She dabbed carefully at where she thought the screws ought to be with paint stripper, until her patience wore out, and she dug the hinges out of the door frame with a crowbar, screws still in place.

She had the radio on for company as she worked. The eye-in-the-sky reported a growing tail back from a burst water main in Gloucester Road. She looked out at the early morning lorries grinding slowly eastwards and wondered, not for the first time, why no-one used freight trains anymore.

She was fitting a new lock when a straggle of women appeared round the corner, trudging tiredly towards her. Torn between running down the steps to greet them and going to put the coffee on, she tried to imagine how she would feel after a night in the nick. No question; she waved sketchily at the little procession and went to fill the percolator.

"Hi Kerry, we're back," Marlene called unnecessarily, as she stumbled into the kitchen with Ruth, Kath and a couple of the others. They collapsed around the table. Kerry hugged and kissed them all in turn, even Ruth.

"Where's the rest of you?" she asked.

"Gone to see what state the old homesteads are in. Too depressing for this hour, I should think," Kath pillowed her head on her folded arms. "Is that coffee I smell?"

"Coming up."

"You're an angel."

"Never mind that, tell me what happened."

Marlene marshalled her thoughts with an obvious effort. "It was the fake Credit Transfer Facilities they were after," she said at last.

"Oh shit."

"They hauled us each in, said they could get us for benefit fraud, or whatever, but they'd let us off if we'd tell them about how the Credit Transfer identities were fixed up."

"I suppose everyone is ripping off the Social one way or another."

"I'm not," said Ruth.

"Aren't you good?" Kath jeered.

"So you didn't tell them anything?" Kerry persisted.

"Of course not." Kath looked around at the others for confirmation. "The strange thing was, they didn't have the faintest idea that they'd actually got nearly all the people who do the false Credit Transfer work there."

"I don't understand," Kerry frowned.

"They used the Benefit enquiries as an excuse to pick us up because we're all involved with groups which have got illegal Credit Transfer Facilities," Ruth explained. "They thought we would tell them who had done the deed."

"But they obviously never thought it could be us who set it all up," Kath agreed.

"In fact," Marlene snorted, "they kept asking me to tell them the names of the men behind it all."

"Silly boys," Kerry tutted.

"Two of them interviewed me," Ruth reflected. "Did anyone work out who the ferrety little number in the two-piece was?"

"Higgin, that's the copper," Kath explained, "told me the other guy was from the Banking Societies Central Security Service."

"That figures," Ruth nodded. "He was the one who asked me all the technical questions about where the Centre spirited its funds away to, when we got turned down by the Banking Society."

"So what have they got against you?" Kerry asked.

Kath shook her head. "Not much. They released some of us without charge even. Most of the Income Assistance fiddles and tax registration would be a fine, if it ever came to court. Marlene probably has the most against her, doesn't she?"

"Yes," Marlene agreed gloomily. "They've matched up some of my previous IDs. And I don't suppose it will take them long to find Gillian Prebble's death certificate, if they look for it. I could go down for a few months, I suppose, if the worst came to the worst."

"They don't know who you really are yet, though, do they?" Ruth rubbed her drooping shoulders.

"Guess not."

"You could do a bunk then," Kerry said briskly, clearing plates and refilling coffee cups. "If Gillian Prebbel vanishes, they're not going to know where to look."

"I never did much care for the name. Not really me somehow."

"You would have to find somewhere else to live," Ruth looked distressed as she said it.

"Yes. Maybe I'll have to go travelling again." There was an unhappy silence. Kerry gave them thirty seconds in which to be broken-hearted about their imminent separation, then stood up, saying, "You don't have to do anything straight away, not until you know whether or not they are going to press charges."

"That's right," Kath encouraged the forlorn lovers.

"And since I have to get to work right now, I wonder if we could sort out a meeting of the Credit Transfer group for tonight, to talk about our security?"

"Do you think we should?" Ruth was dubious. "They may still be watching us. To see who we get together with."

"I think it would look suspicious if we weren't all getting together." Marlene roused herself from her depression. "After all, there is so much coming and going between the houses usually."

"That's true," Ruth conceded. "And maybe if we all rushed about talking to strange men all day, it would throw them off a bit."

"Ugh," Kath shuddered, "What a prospect."

"The things we do for our sisters," Kerry agreed, rapidly stripping off her painting overalls under which she wore her hospital clothes. "This house tonight then?" The others nodded. "Got to dash. See you later."

When they were alone in the kitchen, and Ruth had called in sick to work, Marlene put her arms around the other woman and felt her trembling.

"How are you?" she asked.

"Not good," Ruth shook herself free and sat down again, fidgeting with her watch, turning it round and round on its wristband.

"I saw that bastard coming out of your cell during the night," Marlene straddled a chair facing Ruth. "Was he hassling you?"

"What a euphemism," Ruth picked angrily at a broken fingernail. "Yes, he was 'hassling' me. No, he didn't threaten to rape me, in so many words. He didn't need to. I can't imagine being in a more threatening situation."

"Poor darling," Marlene stroked Ruth's arm. "But you didn't tell him anything?"

"I didn't tell him anything about Carole the Prostitute and her Credit Transfer machine. But then I don't know the woman. Maybe you could have been more helpful. Maybe you would like to tell me exactly what the fuck you've been doing?"

"Oh shit."

"Well?"

"I didn't think you would like it."

"You're so right," spat Ruth.

"It was a one-off, Ruth. I met this woman, she was desperate. You know what happens if they work the streets."

"How dare you?" Ruth sprang to her feet, pushing the chair aside. She stalked around Marlene in a tight circle. "How dare you jeopardize our whole operation for the sake of keeping some men sexually serviced?"

"It wasn't like that," pleaded Marlene.

"Who else knew about it, from the group?" Though she never shouted, Ruth's voice quivered with rage.

"Kerry helped me," muttered Marlene.

"Oh, she would."

"She didn't like it."

"I'm amazed she could see any difference between a Refuge and a brothel."

"Ruth. . ."

"You knew it was stupid, or you wouldn't have kept it secret. And now we'll have the police on our backs. It's only lucky they didn't get any better quality information out of this woman Carole."

"I'm sorry," Marlene hung her head.

"It's so irresponsible," Ruth fumed. "You and Kerry. At least you thought you were doing someone a good turn. I can't understand what Kerry's motives were."

"I honestly don't think that's why they picked us up," Marlene ventured.

"You wouldn't," Ruth snapped.

"Look, I really am sorry. I wasn't to know Carole would tell the police. I mean, any of the women we work for could shop us."

"The idea is," Ruth was icy, "that we trust them."

"Oh come on, we're not that fussy about who we help."

"Don't push it Marlene," warned Ruth.

"Sorry."

"Well, as it happens, I agree that wasn't why they picked us up. It had more to do with us all having connections with groups for which we've done deals. That was stupid."

"We should have thought," Marlene agreed.

"It doesn't mean what you did wasn't a ridiculous risk to run. And for what? A prostitute!"

"Ruth, they've got to live somehow. We can't all be like you."

"You'll have to tell the rest of the group about it tonight." Ruth calmed down, considering.

"It wasn't them I was scared of," Marlene admitted.

"It is going to make it very difficult to argue against a complete close-down."

"Don't you think we should? We were lucky to get off once. . ."

"We're not giving up," Ruth said, grimly. "Not if I have anything to do with it."

* * *

"They know we are involved, but they don't know we are organising it." Kath addressed the meeting crisply, when they assembled that night. It was the fifth time she had made the same point, but the Credit Transfer group tended to have circular arguments. "Obviously this group has to suspend its activities as long as the police are monitoring us."

"It would be pretty stupid not to," one of the Meredith twins agreed. "I think we should pack it in for good."

"And what happens to all the women we've said we would help?" Ruth put in the objection on which the meeting had been held up for the past two hours.

"Do we just leave them in the lurch?"

"It's too risky," Kath persisted. "Our security is a joke – half the women in London know who we are. And what good can we do if we're caught?"

Kerry slumped in a corner of the crowded room and said nothing. She was tired and bored. She knew they would end up closing down the group, at least while they were being watched. There was no other option. But Ruth, and one or two of the others would argue against the inevitable, all the way to the final vote. It made them feel they were doing the right thing. Kerry, who despised purists, kept quiet. Whoever voiced the unpleasant truth, as Kath was doing, took on the status of the group villain for the evening. Still, they all realised what the decision would be. Ruth knew it as well as anyone, it was what made her stand as the guardian of the poor downtrodden so safe. Kerry yawned.

Marlene, sitting opposite, winked at her and smiled. Kerry wondered how she could stand Ruth's self-righteousness. Marlene had always been one for a quiet life when it came to relationships. Lazy but honest. Tolerant, too. Very different from Ruth. It must be love, Kerry decided sadly.

* * *

Leaving the meeting of the Credit Transfer group, Paula climbed down the front steps of the house, supported by Zoe and with Kath in attendance. Paula, like Kerry, had managed to miss the arrests, having gone early to queue for an antenatal check. But she was in her thirty fifth week of pregnancy and could have done without the excitement.

Higgin approached the trio as they reached the bottom of the steps. He was backed up by a uniformed WPC. Letchley hovered.

"Ms Meredith?" Higgin asked. The twins looked at each other.

"Yes?" said Zoe.

"Ms Paula Meredith?" he sounded puzzled.

"That's me," Paula volunteered.

"Sisters, eh?" he glanced from one to the other.

"No, she's my fucking wife, what do you think?" Zoe snapped. Kath shushed her.

"Paula Meredith, I am arresting you for offences against the Families Act, namely that you did procure by deception a pregnancy through artificial insemination and conspired to create a homosexual family relationship. Anything you say may be recorded and used against you. Any refusal to answer questions will be reported to the court at your trial."

The policewoman strapped Paula's hands behind her. She did not resist. The gun dangling from Higgin's belt was not needed to persuade her.

"I have here," Higgin continued, "an order granting the local authority custody of the foetus, made in accordance with the Unborn Child Preservation Measures. You will be taken to the Custodial Labour Unit at HMP Holloway. Your physician has released you into the care of the Prison Medical Officer."

"You get a free caesarian out of this," the policewoman pointed out helpfully.

Zoe held onto her sister, who looked as though she might faint. The policewoman prised them apart, and at an order from Higgin, took Paula to the unmarked car and locked her in the back.

"You bastard," Zoe spat at Higgin, tears in her eyes.

"She's the one who's having a bastard," he pointed at Paula, slumped in the back of the car. "It'll get a decent home, at least."

"Relieving the curse of infertility for some unhappy family," Letchley agreed.

"I hope she didn't get it off a Black man," Higgin remarked, "there's not such a demand for half-breeds."

Kath and Zoe stood helplessly looking at Paula. Higgin did not seem in a hurry to let them go. A fine drizzle began. The streetlight cast its beam from behind Higgin, illuminating the beads of moisture in his coarse sandy hair. Letchley waited, patient as a lizard watching a fly.

"Artificial insemination," Higgin mused. "I don't know why they bother. Do you Letchley?"

"Perhaps it's the only way they could get a baby,"

Letchley ventured. "I mean, who would want to go with them?"

"You're too fussy Letchley," Higgin looked the two women over. "All they want is a sperm injection. Isn't that right girls?" Neither answered him.

"This is purely routine harassment," Letchley explained. "It can go on and on."

"What my friend here means," Higgin put in, "is that he wants you to co-operate. The sooner you do, the better for you."

"Even if we could tell you anything," Kath said carefully "you wouldn't let Paula go. Or let her keep the baby."

"Of course not," Higgin was dismissive. "Homosexuals aren't allowed children. You should be thinking about the next thing I might pick you up for, or the one after that."

"You know, I can't help feeling," Letchley said, "that a woman who has maternal instincts can't really be a lesbian. Perhaps Meredith has simply been denied the opportunity to meet a compatible male."

"You should talk to her about it." Higgin slapped him on the back. "Let's go and book her in. We'll be seeing you girls."

"Is that a threat or a promise?" Zoe asked bitterly.

"Both," Higgin laughed and followed Letchley to the car.

Al stood in the kitchen wondering whether or not to go to school. As she thought, she held the thumb and middle finger of her left hand close to her ear, clicking the nails against each other. It was a habit she had got when her hearing had started to go. The little clicking noise would reassure her that she could still listen, when she woke up in the morning feeling muffled. Now she was not aware of doing it. She couldn't hear the noise her fingers made today. There was a fullness in her head and throat which meant she was getting a cold. The ringing she heard inside her skull was more high pitched than it had been last night. An infection starting up. Automatically, she reached for the antibiotic ear drops which lived in the cupboard over the sink, tipped her head on one side and squeezed three drops into her ear.

She loved the cold feeling of the thick white liquid sliding up against her eardrum. She straightened up, waiting a minute before tilting her head the other way to do her right ear. She was not meant to use the drops without having seen a doctor, but she knew when she needed them.

Despite the drops, the infection got a grip on her and she started to feel seriously ill. She took herself off to bed and lay there sweating throughout the morning. She wished that Donna hadn't had to go out. Her head felt swollen and full. A high pitched zing went through her brain from ear to ear. She could feel the blood thumping sluggishly round where her jaw bone joined her skull. Behind her eardrums pressed a great mass of fluid, rustling like a dammed up crater full of red hot lava. Her ears felt as though someone had shoved blunt nails into them, and was knocking them home with a sledgehammer.

She looked at the clock. She was not supposed to take any more antibiotics for half an hour. There was always aspirin. Putting her feet carefully on the floor, she got up, swaying slightly. Colours ran down the wall, and she had trouble opening the door, which seemed to be waving in an unfelt breeze.

In the bathroom, she found the aspirin bottle and stood with her hips propped on the edge of the sink, trying to get the childproof top open. Her hands couldn't remember how anti-clockwise went, though she was sure her brain was telling them. In the mirror over the sink, her reflection shimmered and jumped at her. When she moved her head, little exploding stars of light popped out from behind her eyelids. Most of the frightening things came with the high temperature. She was almost used to that by now, she told herself. This was just another ear infection.

She gulped down the tablets chased with as much cold water as she could swallow. Al knew she was burning up with thirst, but she couldn't seem to get much water down. She clutched her old dressing gown, with the three bears on the pocket, around her. Shivering and sweating, she shuffled back to her bedroom.

Passing the front door, she saw an envelope lying in the wire basket behind the letter flap. The brown rectangle fixed and held her interest, although it was probably for Donna, and a bill at that. She dragged herself down the hall, balancing against the wall, leaving clammy handprints on the paintwork.

If it wasn't for her, it was about her. She saw that the letter was from the hospital, and did not hesitate to open it. Her thumb, sliding under the flap of the envelope, felt three times its normal size. A green card with her hospital number printed across the top of it, the consultant's name and a ward number. Date and time. She stared at the letters and numbers as they jumbled themselves across the card. It was her appointment for the operation. She looked again at the date and forced herself to try and think, count forwards. Two weeks time. She had to be well in two weeks time, or they wouldn't be able to do the operation, not with an infection going on.

Al shivered suddenly, and realised that she was still standing in the unheated hall, with a draught howling past her. Almost on all fours, she crawled back to her room and climbed into bed. She slipped into an uneasy sleep, and dreamed of teams of elderly men in surgical gowns forcing grommets into her ear drums with mallets.

Letchley was mildly titillated, but shocked. "It's an orgy," he announced, adjusting the image intensifying viewer.

"Oh yeah?" Higgin did not sound impressed. He had spent a lot of time with Letchley.

"Have a look for yourself. First floor window on the left," but he made no move to hand over the viewer. They were in a derelict house opposite the back of the row of women's squats, twenty five metres across the railway tracks. In Marlene's room, the window was covered with a translucent bamboo blind which excluded neither draughts, nor the prying gaze of strangers, but which Marlene, lacking in the womanly graces, had never got around to replacing with curtains. The light was on, and everything in the room was clearly visible to the watchers in the gathering dark.

"They're mucking about," Higgin cast a bored eye in the direction of the house.

"You can say that again," said Letchley, primly.

"They're mucking about."

Letchley tore himself away from the eyepieces long enough to give Higgin a frozen look.

"Old joke."

Letchley turned huffily back to his observations. Kath, a student of the healing arts, was putting her recently-begun aromatherapy course into practice, anointing Marlene's back with a strongly scented concoction of her own. Ruth lounged on the bed beside the prostrate Marlene, awaiting her turn for a massage.

"It's disgusting," Letchley was still glued to the activities on the first floor.

"Shame you have to force yourself to watch," Higgin looked up from the sports page. "In the line of duty."

Letchley didn't answer. He had spent long enough with Higgin to know when he was being teased, which was often. He propped his elbows on the window sill to steady the image intensifier.

"How much longer are you carrying on with this?" Higgin poured himself a drink from his hot-jug.

"Until something turns up. They're being careful at the moment, but they are bound to slip up sooner or later, and lead us to the real organisers of the Credit Transfer fraud."

"I shouldn't think a professional crook would let this lot come within spitting distance, now they know we've got an interest. They've probably cut all contact."

Letchley put down the viewer and turned to face his colleague. "Do you think so?"

"It's a good bet. Wouldn't you?"

"Perhaps." Letchley looked worried. He tugged at the knot of his tie. Higgin was in his usual open-necked shirt, super-abundant chest-hair visible. Letchley suddenly wondered what the other man looked like naked. Furry shoulders, he guessed, with a shudder.

Higgin, who understood Letchley better than the other man realised, undid another button on his shirt. "What you looking at?" he asked, wide-eyed.

"Nothing." Letchley hurriedly picked up the viewer again.

"Go on, I know what you were thinking. I always reckoned you were a bum boy."

"I am not!" squeaked Letchley with indignant emphasis.

"It's nothing to me," Higgin was expansively tolerant. "Policemen fuck anything, didn't you know?"

"A joke's a joke. . ." began Letchley.

"No, it's no problem. I'll give you a quickie if you want."

"No thank you."

"Not that you could stop me if you didn't want." Higgin grinned.

"What are you suggesting?"

"The only difference between you and a woman is you could go off and do it to someone even weaker than you after, and she couldn't."

"Oh, cut it out Higgin," Letchley had belatedly realised that his colleague was making fun of him. Or so he hoped. "We've got work to do."

"God, you're no fun," Higgin grumbled. "And face it, we've hit a dead end here."

"I don't think so."

"Why? Anyone smart enough to organise such a high-class deal, ripping off the Banking Societies, they're going to have the nouse to cut their losses with this bunch."

"Brilliant crimes get found out because of stupid mistakes. You know that. If thieves were consistently intelligent, we'd never catch them. Which is not the case."

"Humph," Higgin's interest in criminology was slight at the best of times. He shifted on his uncomfortable folding stool.

"I have an idea that, although this is a very sophisticated crime, it may not be the work of experienced criminals."

"How do you figure that out?"

"We have been looking for villains who acquired computer skills. Perhaps that's the wrong way to go about it. Maybe it was a computer literate individual or group developing dishonest practices that got this thing up and running."

"So what?" Higgin scratched. These derelict houses were used by dossers, probably lousy. More than one tramp had shuffled up the stairs at night time, seen the two men and wandered off.

"It makes a difference to the way they'll behave. If it is gifted amateurs, they may know all about our systems management, but they will have less idea of ordinary policing. Which makes them vulnerable to this kind of operation, don't you think? Less aware of security?"

"Sounds like it makes it harder, to me," Higgin grumbled. He did not share his companion's enthusiasm for the chase. "Give me time-served pros any day. You know where you are with them. You know what kind of outfit they're involved with, and you know where to pick 'em up when you need to. Nice and civilized. I don't approve of total strangers setting themselves up in the business. Bloody amateurs." He spat.

"It's no good being narrow-minded," Letchley reproved.

"It's no good being bloody anything in this case." Higgin although normally placid, had let the assignment get on his nerves. "We're looking for a needle in a haystack. The only lead you had has turned out to be stuff-all use. And now you turn round and say it could be any of a million faceless bastards in pin-stripe suits set the whole thing up. What are you trying to do, break my heart?"

"I hardly think it could be just anyone," Letchley was frightened but fascinated by the display of rising temper.

"Of course it could. It might just as well be those bloody women."

"Oh no, really," Letchley protested.

"Why not, they've got a computer, haven't they?"

"Everyone does, that's hardly sufficient proof. And the one thing they haven't got, which the organiser of this scheme certainly does, is money. Whoever set up the false Credit Transfer deals is rich by now, that's for sure."

"So why have I been freezing my backside off, watching these no-hopers?"

"Because like me, you have a job to do."

"Not for much longer."

"What?"

"The old man's pulling me off this one. Face it, pal, we're wasting our time here."

"You mean you're giving up?"

"Orders," Higgin shrugged. "I've got to get back to chasing real criminals you know."

"But what about the co-operation we were

promised? My superiors aren't going to like this at all."

"I'm sure they'll take it up through the usual channels." Higgin lit a cigarette and threw the match out of the open window. "Nothing to do with me."

"But I'm certain these women are going to lead us to the architects of the fraud."

"Bollocks. We could watch them till the crack of doom and all they'd lead us to is a load of poxy nightclubs and the odd meeting."

"In whose opinion?" Letchley quivered with rage.

"Mine, my bosses," Higgin waved airily. "In fact, every bugger who's had anything to do with this but your own good self."

"I didn't know criminal investigation was organised on democratic principles," Letchley said, bitingly.

"You can stay if you want. But as of 9 am, Monday, I'm expected back at my desk."

"I'm very disappointed in you."

"Don't give me that. I told you, it's nothing to do with me. I go where I'm sent, like a good boy."

Letchley sniffed contemptuously and returned to his observation. Higgin stood up, folded his fishing stool and newspaper.

"I'll be off then." Letchley didn't bother to answer. "We'll not proceed with the benefit frauds unless you let us know you want us to. Shan't cramp your style," Higgin sneered. "Cheerio." Letchley ignored him. Higgin made his way out of the crumbling house. "Rum bugger," he said to himself looking back.

Over the tracks, Kath finished the back massage, tucked a blanket over Marlene, who was relaxed to the point of sleep, and shook her hands briskly to loosen the negative energy.

"Face or feet?" asked Kath. "I would do your back too, but I've got to practice face and feet as well."

"Face, then," said Ruth. "Feet sounds a bit ticklish. Shall we go downstairs and leave Marlene to sleep? She looks so peaceful."

"Alright." Kath stood up, collecting her bottles of

oils. Leaving the sleeping Marlene, the two women tiptoed out of the bedroom, turning off the light behind them. Letchley was left without a distraction, or a partner, but determined to carry on.

* * *

Ruth and Marlene lay sprawled in front of the television, digesting Sunday brunch. The cat, a moth-eaten tabby, competed with Marlene's hand for a resting place on Ruth's stomach. Marlene, channel hopping, lighted on a photochemical smog alert for central London.

"I thought it looked a bit hazy," she said, lumbering to her feet to close the window. "Perhaps we'd better stay indoors this afternoon, what with your bad chest and everything."

"Very thoughtful of you. I don't suppose the fact that you didn't actually want to go for a walk has anything to do with this sudden solicitude?"

"Not at all," Marlene settled down comfortably again. "You know how fond I am of the great outdoors."

"As seen on wildlife programmes. Don't worry, I'm not going to drag you out to the park through a cocktail of poisonous gasses. It's already given me a headache."

"That's the trouble with all this fresh air and exercise. So unhealthy. We'll just have to stay in and amuse ourselves somehow."

"What's on that's worth watching?" asked Ruth. "This programme's depressing me." The smog alert had been followed by a warning to water consumers in the Wandsworth area that supplies would be suspended from midnight.

"Let's see," Marlene pressed buttons. "The Week in Strasbourg?"

"Boring."

"Racing?"

"No."

"Boxing?"

"Gross."

"Australian soaps? American soaps? A Japanese game show?"

"None of those." Ruth shut her eyes and stroked the cat, which purred thunderously. "What's on the French satellite?"

"A documentary about their crumbling nuclear power stations."

"Oh, terrific."

"There's an interview with our own dear Prime Minister."

"About?"

"Workfree. You know, the scheme to send redundant labourers from Darlington to Dubrovnik."

"No thank you."

"Failing that, there's God on three channels."

"Oh no," Ruth groaned. "I can't bear it. Turn it off. Sundays, I ask you."

Marlene obligingly silenced the tv and curled up beside her lover. "I could go to the shop and get out a video," she offered.

"Don't bother. We can entertain ourselves."

"Like they did in the old days." Marlene scooped the cat up by the scruff of its neck, and deposited it, protesting, onto the floor. "Kerry'll be back soon."

"Unless she goes round to whatsername's."

"Who?"

"You know," Ruth opened her eyes. "The one she had the hots for. The guitarist."

"She went off with the drummer, didn't you know? Another of Kerry's impossible passions."

"Is that why the band's splitting up?"

"Probably. Poor Kerry, she has such a taste for the unobtainable."

"It's been nice having the place to ourselves," said Ruth, foiling the cat's attempts to re-establish itself on her stomach. The cat stalked off, looking hurt.

"It has, hasn't it?"

"Have you thought about moving out?"

"I haven't heard anything more about those benefit charges," Marlene said hopefully. "Maybe they won't take it to court. Perhaps the CPS has lost the file."

"Marlene," said Ruth, sternly, "wishful thinking will get you nowhere. So long as you carry on living here, and using that name, the police can pick you up at any time. It would always be hanging over you."

"I know. I don't really want to deal with it, though."

"You must."

"Must I?"

"Yes," Ruth was definite.

"Would you like a drink?"

"Stop changing the subject. What are you going to do?"

"It's so difficult," complained Marlene. "Since the whole point of moving is to get away from the police, I can't really risk opening up another squat. And trying to find somewhere to rent could take forever, even if I could afford it, which I can't. No wonder I'm discouraged."

"We could get somewhere together."

"What?"

"We could find somewhere to live together. On our own. I'm getting a bit tired of rambling old barns full of bright-eyed young women who all move in and out again at twice the speed of sound."

"I think I'm being proposed to," Marlene laughed.

"Admit it, you've enjoyed having a bit of time alone together as much as I have. The only thing that Kerry and I have in common is an ability to get on each other's nerves. So, unless you feel that the company of a disapproving teenager is an essential part of our relationship, I think we should move out together."

"What a dreadful old bourgeois individualist you are, under that egalitarian front. I'm shocked."

"Well," Ruth said, defensively, "I think it's right that I should move out. After all, I can afford to rent somewhere, so if I leave, it'll free a place in this house for some woman who doesn't have that option available to her."

"Uh huh?"

"Stop looking like that, and tell me yes or no."

"I don't know."

"Of course, if you'd rather not live with me," Ruth sulked, "I'd quite understand."

"Don't be cross," soothed Marlene, "but you've taken me by surprise. I don't know if I'm ready to settle down."

"Will you think about it?" asked Ruth, anxiously.

"Of course. Give me a bit of time to adjust my political sensibilities, and I'm sure I could get used to the idea of living under a roof that didn't leak."

"Well, if that's the only attraction. . ."

"Oh, am I supposed to say I'd live in a hovel, so long as you were there?" teased Marlene. "I thought that's what we were doing at the moment."

"Shit, that sounds like Kerry," Ruth sat up.

"You look terribly conspiratorial. Come back here and give us a kiss."

"Hullo," Kerry shouldered the door open and strode in. "Oh, sorry to interrupt."

"Not at all," Marlene looked up with a smile. "Ruth was just helping me test out my new denture fixative."

Kerry sniffed and slid her bag off her shoulder onto the floor.

"Have a good time at your mum's?" Ruth asked, too brightly.

"It was alright. Dull. Grandad slipped me a ten pound note when no one was looking, and told me to buy myself something pretty. Silly old fool, he's living in the eighties. God knows how much unconverted cash he's got lying about. Too late to get a Banking Society to accept it now."

"There's half a mycoprotein steak-and-kidney style pie in the kitchen, if you're hungry," offered Marlene.

"No thanks. They were having roast mad sheep with all the trimmings at home. It's rather put me off." Kerry kicked off her shoes and sat down. "I didn't see any police about outside."

"As far as we can make out, there's only that one guy from the Banking Societies left," Marlene said.

"Letchley?"

"Yes."

"What happened to the filth?"

"They all pissed off, for some reason," Ruth

explained. "We woke up this morning, and there they were, gone."

"How odd," Kerry was puzzled.

"Maybe not," Ruth disagreed. "What was there for them to see? We haven't been doing anything while they were watching. It was a fishing expedition. They picked us up, and then watched the house to see what they could find out, not because they knew anything for certain. Otherwise, we wouldn't have been let go so easily. I always said we shouldn't over-react."

"So why is this man Letchley still hanging around? Where is he, by the way?"

"In the burned-out house opposite," Marlene pointed out the glint of sunlight reflected off the lens of the viewer protruding from the first floor window of the ruin.

"And what does he want?"

"We don't know," Ruth stood up, brushing cat-hairs from her clothes. She felt undignified sprawled beside Marlene. "Either he didn't get his marching orders yet, or he thinks we're still worth watching."

"Or he's a nut," Kerry shrugged.

"Worst case thinking, sister," Marlene reminded her. "Always credit the enemy with the most sinister motives, then nothing will come as a nasty shock."

"OK, I'm willing. But we ought to do something about this guy. He could get dangerous." Kerry pulled a face.

"He'll be taken care of," said Ruth, confidently.

"How?"

"We have ways," Marlene smirked.

"What are you up to?"

"Can you hack it?"

"What's the score, Marlene? Stop playing games."

"No games, Kerry, this is security. A bit late in the day, perhaps, but we are trying."

"Give me a clue."

"We can get into the Banking Societies computer."

"One of them," Kerry agreed.

"There's no reason why we should stay in one system. And there is one place where all the Banking Societies interface."

Kerry looked puzzled, trying to think her way through the labyrinth of financial institutions.

"I give up. Tell me."

"I'm not allowed to. My lips are sealed." Marlene looked pleased with herself.

"Oh, really," Kerry was infuriated. She tossed her fringe out of her eyes and stalked off, with more than a passing resemblance to the cat.

* * *

Al hunched over the keyboard in her dressing gown and an old scarf. She was well enough for Donna to have started nagging at her to finish off Cheryl Hopkins' bit of business.

"When can I go out, Mum?"

"Not before you've had your operation," Donna bustled about, putting away shopping.

"But I'm better."

"You've got to be, or they won't do it. And I'm not having you go out and pick up a cold and have to go back on the waiting list for another year."

"The child catcher'll come."

"If," Donna stiffened, "the educational welfare dares show his face round here, which I doubt, I'll soon sort him out."

"Only kidding. Mum?"

"What?"

"Have I got to do Cheryl today?"

"I promised her mother you would."

"I'm tired."

"It won't take you long," Donna peered at the text on the screen. "Looks as though you've done half of it already."

"I've got to get a line and put all that into the Social Credit file yet."

"It won't take you long," Donna repeated uneasily.

"I don't think it's fair," Al sulked.

"What isn't?"

"You never asked me whether I wanted to do anything for Cheryl. I don't even like her. You just go around making promises every time anyone asks you."

"I'm not forcing you. I don't see why you begrudge half an hour of your time to help someone out. It's hardly any bother for you, and it means so much to them. It's not as if you had anything else to do."

"I think you should ask me first."

"Julie was in a state. You know how she gets."

"It's always an emergency."

"And so long as I have anything to do with it, you'll always help those you can. You weren't given this talent for your own gratification, you know."

"I'm not saying I won't do it," Al grumbled. "I just don't think you should say I'll do things for people without asking me. It's not fair."

"Life isn't," said Donna automatically.

"I think we shouldn't just help one or two people. What about everybody else who gets left out?"

"You can only do so much," Donna answered uneasily.

"I think it would be better to really mess up the system. At least that would be fair to everyone."

"That's wild talk, Ali. You don't want to take on more than you can handle. Stick to what you know, I say."

"But I'm sure I could work something out. So no-one had a Social Credit rating, or everyone's would be the same." Al sparkled. "Think, Mum, it would be brilliant."

"It's the risks I think about. Just because you've been lucky so far doesn't mean you can treat the system with contempt. Now, why don't you get on with Cheryl's thing?"

"Oh, Mum," Al protested, but Donna had already gone to the other room. Al picked up the keyboard again, looking martyred.

She worked away, wishing her mum would stop finding people who needed their Social Credit rating fixed. Donna's trouble, she decided, was a soft heart. Or head. It had been fun, when she first found out she could do this. Worm her way into the Social Credit system and do what she liked with it. Then she had been doing it for them, or for her aunts, women she knew. Now it was any old lame dog Donna met, or heard about.

She finished giving Julie's blue-eyed Cheryl enough points to go to college, though why she should bother, Al didn't know. She closed the file again and exited from the system. The excitement had worn off a long time ago. Now it was a chore. And she could never say no, it wasn't worth the aggravation.

"Other kids only get made to do the washing up," she said crossly. Donna had taken herself off, but she might hear from the kitchen.

"I'm fucked off with this," Al murmured rebelliously, calling up one of her best war games. She wanted not to be responsible for sorting out the problems of everyone her mum had ever met. She wanted all the nice things Donna wouldn't let her rip off. More than anything, she wanted to be normal.

* * *

Letchley leant on the plastic bar, stained to look like old oak, and ordered a pint and a pizza. The pub was full of young sales teams and Australians. A vast area of tables stretched into the dark recesses of the barn-like saloon.

He collected his drink and numbered ticket representing his supper and found a table. He had got into the habit of coming here in the early evening, when the women he was watching were feeding themselves. It was the only time of day when he could safely predict where they would be, and what they would be doing. The last few days, alone in the derelict building, or in his car in front of the women's houses, had been a bit wearing on his nerves. Still convinced that the women were worth watching, he found he regretted even the oafish Higgin's departure. And although he stayed at his post for hours at a stretch, alternately looking through the viewer and making notes on computer checks he should request, he was still glad of a break.

"Sixty three," bellowed the woman who was shovelling frozen pizzas into the microwave. There was a loud ping from the oven and another convenience was produced. It looked more like a steaming red cowpat than a Margherita, but Letchley wasn't fussy. He unfolded the cloakroom ticket which bespoke his food and hurried back to the bar. He didn't notice Ruth and Marlene come into the pub, walk up to the bar and stand behind him. He was unaware of the keen interest they took in the small plastic card he extracted from his wallet full of ID to pay for the pizza. By the time he had collected his plate and had his card returned debited, they had seen all they needed and were looking bland and innocent.

"Hullo Letchley," Marlene nodded to him amiably. He took a step backwards, surprised and the mock-Victorian bar caught him in the kidneys.

"What are you doing here?"

"Come for a carryout," she indicated Ruth negotiating the purchase of a plastic jugful of bitter. It had a picture of farmworkers in smocks and a plastic cork.

"Oh."

"Enjoy your tea," she beamed at him and taking Ruth's arm, strolled out. He sat down, and tried not to worry about it.

"Well?" The two women walked rapidly back to the house.

"His initials are JC," Ruth abandoned her silent muttering and wrote on the back of her hand with a marker, "account number 2390716."

"And it's the Surrey Provident Banking Society," Marlene contributed. "Can you get into that one?"

"We shall soon find out. But I should think so. Little runt won't know what's hit him."

"Be careful."

Ruth smiled at her fondly. "I shall make with the walking on eggshells routine."

Donna and Al walked through the hospital looking for E Wing, Ward 7. The long, cluttered corridors were floored with a surface that was alternately tacky and slippery. Heaps of dirty bedclothes lay outside the doors of the wards. Bins came crowding out of side rooms into the passageway, overflowing with disposable implements and used dressings. Dozens of people walked quickly to and fro, consultants dressed like stockbrokers, little flocks of medical students. Porters trundled beds around, some with bodies in them, some not. Through the crowds staggered in slow motion the odd figure in dressing gown and slippers, lost between wardlife and health.

They had followed the signs for E Wing and ended up in genito-urinary medicine three times by different routes. Al, who needed to believe that Donna knew how to cope with the hospital even if she didn't, began to feel shaken.

"Why don't you ask someone, Mum? Go on, ask him," she pointed out a nurse stepping into a lift.

"Excuse me," Donna began, approaching the man as he waited for the doors to close.

"Staff only," he snapped. "No patients in this lift. Use the stairs." The doors clanked shut and he was borne away upwards. Donna tried again. She stopped a passing student and showed her the appointment card.

"ENT?" The student scratched her head. "Third floor. It's the front of the block. Go back the way you've come and up past men's surgical," she smiled and clattered off.

Al scuttled along, her sports bag full of night-clothes tangling in her short legs. She got to the ward and stopped, hopping about, waiting for Donna to catch up.

Long rows of beds stretched away either side of the door. The windows looked over the car park, and to the right there was a view of the incinerator tower. Just inside the door, in a small glass cubicle, the ward sister sat, reading medical notes. Donna walked up and rapped her knuckles softly on the door of the tiny office.

"Yes?" The nurse had no expression but tiredness in her face.

"Alison Treece," Donna used her dealing with officials voice, toneless and precise. "Here for an operation."

"Is that you?"

"Her," Donna gestured at Al. The nurse consulted a list on her wall.

"We'll have to find you a bed then, won't we?" She smiled a small smile at Al and showed them a couple of fold-down seats, attached to the wall. Leaving them perched, she hurried off to where an ancillary was working her way along the empty beds, stripping off the bedclothes. Donna saw her shake her head, pointing to the empty, unmade beds. The nurse returned, looking exasperated.

"The laundry haven't delivered any sheets today, there's a bit of a hold up," she announced. Al and Donna waited, both staring at different bits of the opposite wall. "I'll take the details then, shall I?" Al was being unco-operative, so Donna answered all the questions, date of birth, name of general practitioner, allergies, religion. Al sat and felt as though she had vanished, while the two women talked across her.

The ward sister finished taking notes and tagged Al's wrist with a plastic name strip. She was shown to a bed, with the curtains pulled round, and told to get undressed and into her pajamas. She folded her clothes into the little metal locker and climbed under the covers. The sheets were made of paper, rough, thin and crumpling already.

Another, younger, nurse pulled back the curtains and smiled brightly at Al. She drew a thermometer out of its cotton wool padded holster on the wall and took Al's temperature.

"I'm not ill," Al protested.

"Don't talk," the nurse looked at the watch pinned on her chest.

"What's the point of being in bed when I'm not ill?"

"Sh."

"It's silly," Al rolled the glass tube around under her tongue. The ward was half full, she saw. In the next bed lay a middle-aged woman with a tube sticking out of her neck. She was asleep. Past her was another woman sitting reading a magazine and eating grapes. Al tried to guess what was wrong with her. The domestic had given up waiting for the laundry and was knocking dust off the radiators.

"She's had an infection recently, has she?" the nurse asked Donna.

"She's over it now," Donna answered cautiously.

"Mr Entwhistle will be round this afternoon. He'll see her then." She pulled the thermometer from under Al's tongue, read it, shook it, made a note on the chart at the bottom of the bed.

Al stretched out in her bed and pulled the blankets up to her chin. The blankets were cellular, and too light. The cover too, pale pink and thin might have been made of paper for all she could tell. Donna left, other people came and stood over her, asking each other questions about her.

Al lay and stared at the ceiling. Something about being in a hospital bed all day, doing nothing, made her feel ill and lethargic, although she had been fine when she came in. The women who were waiting for operations sat at the far end of the ward, chatting to each other. The ones who had had operations, or were in with illnesses lay moaning with pain and discomfort. The two nurses rattled round with the medications trolley. They gave Al yellow capsules in a plastic beaker. She swallowed them without asking what they were.

It was dark outside, the windows large squares of black in the wall. The nurses sat in the office with the door open, talking quietly. Al started to drift off. One of the pre-ops shuffled by in her too-large slippers to the bathroom, clutching a sponge bag. Another woman followed her, and Al, blinking in and out of sleep, saw her tuck a packet of cigarettes into the rolled up sleeve of her dressing gown.

"They wanted to put me down on obs and gynae," one of the nurses took off her shoes and rubbed her feet. "But I said, 'no way'."

"Why not?" Her companion was writing up notes in the light of a small desk lamp. The pool of brightness made her face invisible.

"It's the terminations. I can't be doing with it."

"Didn't know you could pick and choose."

"I'm a catholic. It's the conscience clause. They can't make you."

"Doesn't bother me."

"Well, it's more the mess than anything that gets me. And they lie there crying afterwards. Depressing."

"I had to stand in on male psycho-geriatric last week. It's not right, I said, I'm not trained for it, but you know how it is."

Al watched the nurses sleepily. She saw the women come back from the bathroom and get into bed. The air conditioning hummed and clattered, but she felt too hot. She wriggled out of her pajama bottoms and laid them beside her under the bed-clothes. She would have liked to take the top off too, but it felt awkward. The main lights had been switched out, but you could still see all the beds. Al put her hands outside the bed to cool the blood at her wrists and fell uneasily asleep.

* * *

Kerry felt the sweat run down the side of her face and drip off her chin. The coloured lights shone hot; through the glare she could make out the general heaving that looked like a whale beached in the night which was two hundred women dancing in a small space. Under her feet, the precarious stage flooring flexed up and down.

By-oom ba da, and three, and four, she counted to herself. Her lip buzzed and trembled with playing loud. The woman on the sound desk was losing her in the mix. She stood to one side of the stage with the rest of the horn section, two saxes and a flugelhorn, watching the gaffa tape that was holding her mike together slowly unpeeling itself in the heat.

A final, neat, crashing flourish from the drum machine, the song was over. Some applause, nothing ecstatic, they were only warming up for the star band. At least they were dancing, that was a minor bloody miracle.

The tenor sax bent to look at the set list taped to the floor by the monitor. "Jesus Christ," she muttered, sweat dripping off her onto the already soggy paper. "I can't remember what key we're playing this next one in."

"Concert A," Kerry said, out of the corner of her mouth, blowing water out of her trombone.

"Shit, what's that if you're in B flat?" the woman's stage fright always affected her memory. She started counting on her fingers.

The singer finished her long, rambling introduction to the next song and started tapping her foot to count them in. She looked around the band and nodded to the guitar who had the opening bar. Kerry took a breath, pushed out her diaphragm like a life belt round her middle and forced the air down deep. She wished she could let out another notch on her belt, but her trousers were only just holding up as it was.

Now her eyes were used to looking across the lights, she could see Ruth and Marlene propping up the side of the hall, draped over each other like they so often were these days. She wished they hadn't turned up tonight. She had heard them talking about a flat they had been to see together. That was one of the disadvantages of sharing with a pair, the obviousness of their secrets and the suspicion that, when they lowered their voices and put their heads together, they were talking about the household singleton. Kerry wondered when they would tell her that they were moving out, and whether she should pretend to be surprised.

When they left, she would have to go through the whole tedious business of learning to live with strangers who wanted silence in the mornings, kept terrapins and were lovers with women she wasn't speaking to. But that wouldn't worry Ruth and Marlene, she thought bitterly, watching them flaunt their happiness. Wishing that she had been less insistent that they buy tickets to her band's farewell performance, she slapped her foot on the floor to keep time and tried to remember whether she had said she would take a solo on the next number.

* * *

Al came out of the anaesthetic furiously angry. She lay on the trolley coming from the recovery room and wanted to hit someone, but didn't know why.

The porter, who was wheeling her back to the ward, pushed her into the lift. He pressed the 'doors closed' button and the lift clanked slowly upwards. The porter whistled quietly between his teeth, and Al lay, staring up at the thick black hairs that grew out of his nostrils. Also on the back of his hands, she saw. He looked down at her, and seeing she was awake, grinned and winked.

"You'll be alright now, kid," he said kindly.

Al didn't answer. She saw his lips move. As though she hadn't noticed it before, an intense roaring filled her ears. Through the last shreds of anaesthetic came the start of a dozen sharp pains, worse than any earache she had had. Convinced that the operation had failed, that they had slit open her eardrums and left her totally deaf, Al started to cry.

Marlene slung the old netting hammock between two plane trees in the jungly garden and climbed in cautiously. The ropes stretched and sagged, but held. She swung with her curved back brushing the impacted mud which served as a lawn, and one leg trailing over the side. Ruth sat cross-legged beside her, pushing gently off every time the hammock swung to a stop. Hot early summer sun fought through the green mass of leaves overhead and raised a stuffy fug in the dank, unweeded garden.

"He's not there, is he?" Ruth squinted up at the derelict house across the tracks.

"Nor out the front," Marlene agreed, smugly.

"You think it worked?"

"Darling, that was one of your finest creations." Marlene planted her bare foot against Ruth's shoulder and pushed herself off. "In and out the Banking Societies network like it was the dusky bluebells. Making sure his number came up for a 'routine' security check. Backdated credit and debit entries. That's the touch of true artistry. The debits."

"It was lucky I could get from our tame, hackable Banking Society into the Central Security System, where they all interface for networked account policing."

"Lucky nothing. It was pure inspiration."

"OK," Ruth admitted, "it was neat work."

"Neat work!" Marlene tried to sit up, but the hammock clutched her. "Is that all you can say in the face of your own true genius? You're a craftswoman."

"I'm glad it came off."

"Maybe you should go back into assertiveness training."

"Goddess forbid," Ruth pulled a long, tough grass and chewed the stalk.

"Kerry's furious that she wasn't in on it."

"Sour grapes. She'll get over it."

"We should give them an answer today. About the flat."

"What do you think?"

"Seemed OK to me."

"I liked it."

"Well then," Marlene pushed off again and swung, "let's tell them we'll have it."

"We?"

"It was your idea to live together. I guess you do still want to."

"I do," Ruth knelt beside the hammock, so that she could look at Marlene's face. "I wasn't sure that you were decided though."

"I decided," Marlene smiled at her. "It frightens the shit out of me, but I'll give it a try. Try anything once."

"You're so kind," Ruth pulled a face.

"Well, I've got to move out of here, you don't. So I suppose you're taking more of a risk than me. But I won't know if I can handle it until I've tried."

"Like picking up spiders."

"I like spiders."

"There you go then." Ruth stood up, her knees cracking. "We'll have to tell Kerry tonight."

"She'll be pissed off. About the two of us going together."

"About you, maybe. She'll hardly miss me."

"Oh well," Marlene shrugged and climbed out of the netting, landing in a heap at Ruth's feet, "it won't be as hard as deciding who carries who over the threshold of our new home."

* * *

The head of the Banking Societies Central Security Service shook his head sadly. "It came as quite a shock to me, I don't mind admitting."

"How did you come across the information? Sir." Higgin added the "sir" as an afterthought. The guy might be a civilian, but he had a lot of clout, there was no doubting that.

"A routine check," the man waved his hands over the several square yards of walnut-veneered desktop. "We examine the personal accounts of our employees as a security measure. On a random basis, unless there is a particular reason for suspicion."

"And was there? In this case?"

"No, I believe the man's name was simply coughed up by our computer as part of the latest batch to be checked."

"He's been taking payoffs?"

"That is the only possible explanation. Large influxes of credit over the last six months from an illicit source. We haven't been able to trace the paymasters any further back than their cover, but the Credit Transfer identity which they are using is false."

"And debits? What's he been spending it on?" Higgin wished the man would offer him a chair. He felt like a wine-waiter, hovering with his note recorder.

"Gambling clubs mostly," the security chief looked shocked. "I had no idea."

"No history of it?"

"Certainly not."

The communications centre on the desk buzzed. Higgin watched the other man press the button and heard a secretary's voice announcing "Mr Letchley to see you, sir."

"Very well, send him in."

The door opened and Letchley strode across the large expanse of carpet in front of his boss's desk.

"I believe you wished to see me, sir?" he stood almost to attention in front of the desk. If I'm the wine-waiter, thought Higgin, he's the manager. And the old guy, a particularly difficult customer.

"Yes I did, Letchley. You know Detective Sergeant Higgin, I gather?"

"Certainly," Letchley turned and gave Higgin a thin smile, as though he had not noticed his former colleague's existence, until it was officially pointed out. "Although I understood that co-operation from that quarter had been withdrawn."

"Jason Charles Letchley," Higgin intoned with a blank expression, "I am arresting you on suspicion of fraud, corruptly receiving bribes and conspiring to pervert the course of justice."

Letchley goggled at him. "This is no place for your puerile sense of humour, Higgin," he said sternly. "I presume you have come here to discuss the Credit Transfer case, so don't waste the chief's valuable time with these pleasantries."

Higgin fished the warrant out of his pocket and handed it silently to Letchley. The look of irritated indignation on Letchley's face changed as he read. He looked from the po-faced Higgin to the head of the Security Service, rocking gently in his swivel chair, and his jaw sagged.

"What is the meaning of this?" he demanded.

"We have examined your personal account," his boss said sternly, "and observed the large sums of money you have been receiving over the last few months. Bribes, we can only conclude. From the organisers of the false Credit Transfer racket. The notably unsuccessful investigation of which, you have been leading. Astray, it now appears to us."

"This is a monstrous speculation. Absurd." Letchley felt his palms sweating and put his hands in his pockets.

"You have betrayed our trust, Letchley."

"It's a lie."

"The figures don't lie. There is all that credit going into your account. So much more than you earn here."

"I demand to see the record. I've had no credit that I didn't earn at this job. Someone has falsified the record. That's it," he looked at the other two, as though expecting them to see the reason of it and apologize.

"Do me a favour, Letchley," Higgin yawned ostentatiously. "Come up with something a bit creative, can't you? That line hasn't even got novelty value."

"I've been framed," Letchley said, amazed.

"Oh, really," Higgin sounded exasperated, made a quick tossing gesture with his right hand. "Who by?"

Letchley stared at Higgin, thinking hard. He opened and shut his mouth a few times, frowning. The policeman gave him eight on ten for trying, five on ten for acting skills. He'd seen better.

"It's those women," Letchley burst out at last. "Of course, I should have seen it at once. They've set me up, because they know I'm the only one who poses any threat to them."

Higgin sneered and the head of Security drummed his fingers.

"Don't be ridiculous," he snapped. "We realise now why you have been trying so hard to concentrate the investigation on those wretched harpies, to the exclusion of all else."

"It must be them," Letchley looked thunderstruck. "It stands to reason."

"What stands to reason," Higgin lumbered in, patiently, "is that you had us chasing those women to keep us away from the real perpetrators."

"Protecting your paymasters," agreed the other man repressively.

"It's not true," Letchley came out of his reverie and realised the alarming predicament in which he stood.

"Don't waste my time," Higgin moved closer to Letchley, menacingly.

"We are prepared," the chief steepled his fingers and peered over them, "under certain circumstances to consider making an accommodation with you."

"What?" Letchley stared at him blankly.

"He means, give us the name of the bloke who's paying you off, and who's running the Credit Transfer fiddle, and they might not press charges."

"But I can't, don't you see?" Letchley wrung his hands and writhed with frustration. "The fact that I have been made a target like this proves the investigation must have been along the right lines."

"You are doing yourself no good, Letchley," his boss warned sternly.

"Be a bit sensible," agreed Higgin. "The nice man made you an offer."

"I have nothing to tell you. Can't you get it through your thick head that I have been made a scapegoat?"

"Nasty," Higgin tutted. "And I thought you and me were friends."

"And I thought you were an oaf," Letchley snapped, "from the day I met you. This merely confirms it."

"I don't think he's going to co-operate," a look of distaste crossed the face of the head of Security. "Perhaps you could take him away and pursue this elsewhere?" He looked hopefully at Higgin.

"Certainly sir," Higgin grasped Letchley by the arm and steered him towards the door. "Come along now." Letchley shook himself free and stalked forwards on his own. Higgin cast an apologetic smile over his shoulder at the other man, and followed in his prisoner's indignant wake.

Al vaulted over the low wall around the park. Her arm trembled at the sudden weight. She didn't understand why she should still feel so weak. She was better now, after all. Donna had made her promise to stay indoors today, not to go out and risk catching something. It might set her back, Donna said. But the sun was hot, beating down on the concrete box of the flat, making it airless. And she had spent enough time sitting around at home getting over the operation. Added to the time lying in hospital.

Sound crackled around her, each new noise a surprise. Dogs barked and yapped, chasing each other across the grass. Toddlers screamed in the paddling pool. She could hear the hum of traffic on the road outside and the clatter of a pneumatic drill where they were digging up a gas main. The only sound she couldn't hear was the roaring and ringing of tinnitus. Before, the inside of her head had been full of noise, with the quiet outside. She felt as though her ears had been turned inside out. The world was reversed.

Deliberately, she walked close to people who were talking, eavesdropping on their conversations. Two women pushed small children in buggies along the tarmac path that cut the park in two.

"The health visitor kept on at me about how simple it was to express milk and all that. But I couldn't be messing about. Put him on a bottle in the end. Simpler."

"They say it's bad for them."

"He's putting on weight alright."

"I read somewhere they're more likely to get divorced if you don't feed them yourself. You know, emotionally stunted."

"Oh yeah?"

"What it said."

Al jogged off from the path grinning to herself. Her shoes made a crunching noise on the dry grass and beech mast. She picked up a twig and broke it in two for the pleasure of the snap. She stuck her hands in her pockets and whistled, walking with her biggest stride. The wail of police sirens rose and fell along the road. A jet lumbered overhead. Far across the park she could hear the thud and yells of bigger kids playing football.

"Man on you, Jeff."

"To me, Mervin. Pass, you bastard."

A man lay on the bench in front of her. A bottle of British sherry stuck out of the pocket of his old trenchcoat. Plastic bags held up with string covered his feet. More plastic bags lying beside the bench held his portable home: newspapers, cardboard and wads of cotton waste. He lay on his side, with his head raised awkwardly and stared at Al with red-rimmed eyes.

"It's the work of the devil, you are," he hissed. "You'll see, on the last day, when Satan claims his own, then you'll know I was right. Jezebel." He spat at Al, who stood in front of him, out of reach. He propped himself on his elbow and whispered on, spitting and wheezing.

"Evil and wickedness. You too, don't think you can escape. Out of the mouths of babes and sucklings. What are you fucking grinning at? Go back to hell, go on and burn, you all will," he glared at Al and took a pull of sherry, dribbling a brown stain into his beard. Carefully, she backed away, taking the smile off her face.

* * *

Kerry hummed to herself as she set up the equipment for her last patient. The end of the day, the end of the week. She would go out tonight, she decided, and have a proper Friday evening on the town. She stuck her head out of the corridor to call the last bit of work.

"Alison Treece."

Al sat alone in the line of chairs which had sagged all day under the weight of a hundred frustrated patients. She heard Kerry call her name, jumped to her feet and strolled along to the test room.

"Hi, Al. How are you?"

"OK," Al didn't elaborate, but she smiled. "I hoped it would be you."

"Did you? You still off school?"

"No," Al pulled a face.

"Don't you like it?"

Al mimed retching. "Hate it. They got me in the thicko hut."

"The what?"

"Slow learner unit, or remedial teaching class, or whatever they're calling it this week."

"But why are you there?"

"Must be thick, mustn't I?"

"Oh yeah?"

"Yeah. Anyway, I don't always go," she looked defiantly at Kerry.

"You bunk off?"

"Uh huh."

"I used to. When I was at school. Hated it there too."

"Don't tell mum," Al sized up Kerry's trustworthiness.

"I won't. Where is your mum, anyway? I thought she usually came with you."

"She had to go to work, and they wouldn't change the time of the appointment. So I've come on my own."

"It's a long way."

"Sure," Al agreed, then realised the implication of Kerry's remark. "I'm not a baby. I go out on my own all the time."

"I wasn't suggesting you didn't." Kerry changed the subject quickly. "Do you want to stick on those headphones and we'll do your ear tests. Mr Entwhistle doesn't like to be kept hanging about. Especially not on Friday afternoons, when he's got his weekend cottage in Norfolk waiting for him."

"OK," Al hopped up onto the stool and hung the headphones around her neck. "Ready when you are."

Kerry left the soundproof booth, shutting the heavy door behind her. She reappeared the other side of the window and gestured to Al to put the headphones over her ears and press the response button to test it.

The series of tones ran quickly down the wires. Al, frowning with concentration, pressed the button when one frequency became audible, then another. The whining tones moved over to the other side of her head as Kerry tested the other ear. A couple of minutes later, Kerry vanished from her desk in the other room and reappeared at the door of the sound booth.

"That's it."

"Do I have to go and see Mr Entwhistle now?"

"'Fraid so."

"Kerry?"

Kerry jumped a bit at the use of her name, "Yes?" Al was looking at her sideways, considering something.

"Would you do me a favour?"

"Depends what it is."

"You're sharp, aren't you?"

"No flies on me," Kerry agreed, good humouredly.

"Will you wait for me and tell me how things really are. You know he never tells you anything."

"Alright," Kerry looked surprised. "I'll be tidying up round here. Come back when you're through with his majesty."

Al stood up and made for the door. "Thanks." She vanished. Kerry pottered about putting things away. All the other staff had gone already, on the basis that if you didn't have a patient booked in, you made yourself scarce for the last half of Friday in case the devil, or the consultant, found work for your idle hands. She didn't think Al would be very long, Entwhistle never knew what to say to kids on their own. She took off her overall and got her coat. Unplugged all the instruments and turned out the light. She was waiting in the corridor when Al came bouncing back.

"Let's get out of here," she said.

"Aren't you going to tell me?" Al looked hurt.

"I said I would, didn't I? But this department closes at five o'clock. Security will come and lock us in, if we don't hop it. And I don't know about you, but I can think of more fun places to spend the weekend."

"Don't they open it again until Monday?"

"No. So come on." Kerry led the way to the lifts.

"Where are we going?"

"There's a caff over the road. We could go there, if you like, and I'll buy you a cup of tea." They were sinking down to the entrance floor in the staff lift. Together they made their way through the foyer.

"Where do you live?" asked Al.

"Not far from here."

"How far?"

"Ten minutes walk maybe. Why?"

"We could go back to your house. For a cup of tea."

"My god, if you were a few years older, I'd think you were cruising me."

"What's that?"

"Never mind," Kerry stood at the hospital's main door and thought. "Yes, OK. I doubt if there's anything immoral going on in the old place."

"Is there usually?"

"You never can tell." Kerry set off briskly. They walked most of the way in silence.

"Here we are," she opened the front door of the house. "Home, sweet home, be it ever so humble and all that." Al was looking around her, wide eyed, but trying not to show it.

"Looks like it was empty. You know, like no-one lived here."

"That's because the basement's boarded up. Now don't be rude about the old tip, it's all I've got."

"I wasn't," Al followed her down the hall, raising an eyebrow in passing at the posters, and into the living room. "Anyway, you are. Rude about it."

"That's different. I live here. I'm allowed to be rude about my own home. Nobody else is."

Al wandered over to the entertainment centre. "Can I put on some music?"

"Sure," Kerry went to fill the kettle. "What do you want? Tea or coffee?"

"Coffee." Al knelt in front of the racks of discs and tapes, reading the titles. "Milk and sugar," she looked over her shoulder and smiled at Kerry. "Please."

"So polite, all of a sudden," Kerry marvelled, going to the kitchen to fetch milk. When she came back, she found Al listening to one of the band's rehearsal tapes, and groaned.

"What's the matter?" Al took her coffee and sat cross-legged in front of a speaker.

"Of all the things to play."

"What is it?"

"A band I was in, practising our greatest hit."

"Which one is you?"

"The trombone. Listen," Kerry hummed the bass line of the horn section, blaring and slurping over the crackles in the tape.

"I think it's good."

"Turn it off, will you? It brings back unhappy memories."

"Will you play something for me? On your trombone? I've never seen anyone play one." Al looked appealing.

"Maybe. I thought you wanted to hear about your tests?"

"Go on then," Al sighed. "I'm not sure I do, but tell me anyway."

"How long is it since you had the operation? A month?"

"About that. Why?"

"You've still got some hearing impairment. Know what that means?"

"Of course I know. But I can hear fine."

"Not perfectly though. What I'm saying is that what you have now is a whole lot better than the state things were in before, but you don't have perfect hearing."

"Will I ever have perfect hearing?"

"You could do. Your own tubes should be able to drain the fluid out of your ears properly. When they do that, when they heal, the grommets are pushed out."

"How long does that take?" Al crossed her legs tighter and folded her arms, making herself small.

"Six months, maybe a bit longer. If everything isn't working properly by then, they could do the operation again, put new grommets in," Kerry saw the girl's face lengthen and hurried on, "but I shouldn't think you would need that. You seem to be doing alright."

"It terrifies me sometimes you know. If I wake up feeling a bit thick in the head, and think 'Oh no, here we go.' And knowing I could have to go through all that again. It feels brilliant, because it's so much better than it was. But sometimes I think it's going again a bit, then I get depressed."

"Al, it's an operable condition. You're not going to be deaf."

"Why couldn't Mr Entwhistle have said that?"

"What did he say?"

"Fuck all, really. Rabbited on about 'how was I doing in school?' and 'not to worry, everything would be fine.' You know."

"Yes, well, he doesn't believe anyone could understand about their own bodies. He is the expert, after all."

"He's a bastard."

"You're so right. Mind if I smoke?"

"Not if you give me one."

"I don't think I should be encouraging you."

"I don't need your encouragement," Al stuck out her chin and screwed up her freckles in a frown.

"Look, Al," Kerry tried to retrieve her position. "It's none of my business what you do. But I don't want to be in the situation where your mum or anyone could say I've been corrupting you."

"Why should they?"

"It's the sort of thing people say about women like me around younger people."

Al gave her a hard stare and let it pass. She unfolded herself from the floor and walked over to the computer, whose shape she could make out under its chenille cover. Without asking, she uncovered it, sat down and booted the system. Kerry came and stood behind her, watching over her shoulder. Al glanced at the programme copyright information.

"You got one yourself?" Kerry watched her find her way quickly through the options.

"Mine's a crappy old thing. And I can't use the modem half the time, 'cos the 'phone keeps getting cut off, and mum won't let me fix the bill," Al spoke absently, her fingers busy with the keyboard. Kerry's interest was caught.

"How would you fix it?"

"Oh, you know. Put some credits into our account file," Al was offhand and preoccupied.

"You a hacker?"

Al looked over her shoulder. "I never said that."

"I just wondered," Kerry studied for casualness, "I'm quite interested in that sort of thing myself."

"You do it?"

They looked at each other, weighing up how much they could say.

"Look," Kerry broke the silence. "We hardly know each other, and I guess you're thinking 'is it safe to tell this woman I break this law and that law, when she could go and shop me for all I know?'"

"And you're thinking, 'I can't trust her, she's just a kid.'"

"That's about it," Kerry agreed. "But we could see it as mutual blackmail, if we don't know enough to trust each other. So if we both admit that we break into other people's systems, then I have as much over you as you do over me. And neither of us is going to say anything."

"OK," Al accepted warily. "Can I do a bit of timesharing on your hardware? I need to sort out our 'phone bill. Mum won't find out right away."

"Sure. Help yourself," Kerry waved at the computer, relieved. "But don't use that 'phone."

"Why not?"

"It's tapped. Special Branch can trace any number you dial on it."

"How do you get a line then?" Al frowned.

"We have another 'phone." Kerry rummaged in the cupboard under the bookshelves and produced a strange looking one-piece machine. "We made it ourselves. It's not an officially registered number, so there's no reason for them to put a tap on it. It's an untraceable mobile access unit. Pirates Aircell. They might pick up the signals accidentally if they were microwaving for something else in the neighbourhood, but it's a small chance. And we don't use any of the key words or numbers that would set the tapes rolling at Menwith Hill." She placed the second 'phone in the rest, with the digits facing upwards. "It's all yours."

Al grinned at her, then dialled a number. She got a line and negotiated the security block at the second attempt. It took her five minutes to find Donna's account file and credit it. Kerry watched with professional interest.

"You've done this before," she said, as Al logged off.

"Not with this system. But they're all pretty much the same shape. When you know your way round one. . ."

"It only needs a little bit of logic to work out your way round them all."

"Yes."

"Still want that cigarette?" Al nodded and stood up. Kerry took her place in front of the screen. "And now," she said, "before you show me what you do for an encore, you can watch some of my work."

Kerry opened the Credit Transfer file she was working on, to be ready for when the group gave the all clear to get their operations back to normal. She inserted fictitious details busily. Al watched over her shoulder, silently following every move she made. Kerry felt she had at least to match the quick deftness with which Al had worked. She rattled through with flourishes and fancy short cuts to impress the girl.

"You're into Credit Transfer scams?" Al leaned on the back of her chair, observing her exit from the work.

"As you can see. And a major breach of security it

it is too, letting you watch like this. As if I wasn't the one always going on about secrecy."

"Stuff that. I thought we had mutual blackmail going on?"

"You don't worry me that way Al."

"No reason why I should." Al leaned over her shoulder and hit a few keys. "It's nice to be able to have a conversation with the back of your head."

"Must be," Kerry moved aside. "Delightful though a woman's lips may be, it's better if you can watch other of her moving parts, while chat is going on."

"Hmm." Al looked at her sideways. "So you do CT. Me, I'm mostly into Social Credit."

"It's all the same system."

"No it's not."

"Political system, I mean. It's all about controlling who gets what."

"Oh yeah. Pretty fucked then, isn't it?"

"Too right." Kerry got up and let Al have the keyboard. "How did you start?"

"Hacking?"

"Yes."

"I was mucking about. A year ago. Bored, you know. I'd been ill, stuck indoors for two weeks with no-one for company. I started playing around with my Social Credit number. Unscrambling it."

"Why?"

"Something to do. I like the patterns numbers make. Anyway, I could see it was a jumbled up version of my birth-date and initials. Plus a few other digits."

"Representing?"

"An area code for the district I was born in, and a 2 for female. It's 1 for males."

"A sort of anagram?"

"Yes. And if you can work out which piece of information transfers to where in the Social Credit number, you can crack the encryption of Social Credit programmes. So when you hack into one of their files, instead of a screenful of garbage you can get a plain text that makes sense."

"Handy. Was it that easy?"

"I messed around with it for days. Got Donna to find out the birthdays and Social Credit numbers of some friends. She thought it was a game at first."

"Then what?"

"I told her I could get us uprated. She threw a wobbler. Forbade me to input any data to our files or alter the rating."

"Why?"

"Who knows. She's got her principles. They're a bit of a pain, my mum's principles."

"What changed?"

"Oh, I kind of wore her down. About the operation, which was the thing I wanted most. She couldn't really say no to that in the end. But the only other thing she would let me do is get my school changed. For a 'nicer' one." Al grimaced.

"Why don't you?"

"Not interested. The only useful thing I ever learnt at school was how to pick locks. Don't suppose they do much of that at the grammar."

"Seems daft to me," Kerry scratched her head, "that you should have found your way into the Social Credit system and your mum stops you doing anything about it."

"Oh no," Al sneered. "She doesn't stop me. She's always bringing me little chores to do. Good deeds. So long as she feels we're helping someone out. So long as it's nothing crass, like making ourselves comfortable and well-off. I'm a sodding charity, you know that?"

"I don't understand."

"No more do I. But she's pig-headed and pious with it."

"A bad combination."

"You said it."

"But though your mum sounds like a bit of a trial, it's not really her that's the problem. It's the system, like I said. The way things are organised."

"Well, someone ought to do something about it. Fuck things up for them," Al played with the computer as she spoke.

"'Them' as in the powers that be?"

"Uh huh."

"You and I do our humble best, don't we?"

"That's the trouble. Humble, isn't it? I get the odd widow and orphan rehoused. What about you?"

"The women's organisations we help may not be large, but they are important," Kerry threw herself down in the corner.

"But there are more people getting done over than we could ever help."

"So what? You want to give up? Doing a little is better than doing nothing at all." She hunched her shoulders truculently.

"No, not that." Al frowned. "Sometimes I just get sick of running around after all these small disasters. One kid into college here. Someone else onto a hospital waiting list there. It doesn't change anything."

"For the women you help, surely?"

"Oh yes," Al agreed, dismissively. "A little bit of fair play in a lifetime of getting screwed. But every time I put someone ahead in the queue, someone else has to wait longer. Someone I don't know."

"What do you want to do?" Kerry was uncomfortable at Al's bitterness. "It may not be perfect, but at least we do even things up a bit. Between the haves and the have-nots."

"That much," Al held her index finger a millimetre away from the ball of her thumb.

"Are you calling me a reformist, you wicked brat?"

"Come again?" Al looked aggressively blank.

"Accusing me of making small rearrangements in the ordering of hell. So what do you want to do instead?"

"Stop faffing about on the edges of things. We can't make the system, if that's what you call it, better. So let's do as much damage as we can."

"Drastic," Kerry murmured.

"Me, I'm just a vandal," Al grinned. "I'm sick of being the nice little girl who does good deeds for the neighbours."

"Vandals smash up 'phone boxes, darling. What

you're talking about could have us both in the Tower of London till the ravens fly home."

"It's my deprived background," Al smiled. "There's no 'phone boxes round our way to smash."

"What would you do?"

"To wreck things?"

"Yes," Kerry mused. "It would be nice to wipe all the data in the Social Credit files."

"Physically?" Al wrinkled her nose. "Difficult."

"You could drape a co-ax cable across the building and pass current through it. The electro-magnetic field would wipe anything stored in magnetic media."

"Bit untidy, isn't it? You'd need a few people to haul the cable into position. Bound to be noticed."

"What about introducing a voltage spike into the main supply?"

"Nope. There's a regulator at the substation. You'd need a massive bloody transformer to get a surge through that. Your trouble is you go about things the wrong way, Kerry." Al's eyes gleamed.

"So women keep telling me."

"You picture an attack with some bunch of heroes in balaclavas hefting technical gizmos around the rooftops."

"So?" Kerry blushed, "I watched too many action videos as a kid."

"So, nothing. Most of the protection the Social Credit computer has got is against damage from the outside. You've got to get inside it, compromise its integrity. Make it destroy itself."

"How about a small thermonuclear explosion," Kerry offered hopefully. "That would wipe the files."

"Wouldn't it just? Be practical, Kerry."

"OK," Kerry admitted defeat. "Tell me how you would do it."

"Well," Al drummed her fingers. "It's a networked database system, yeah? Any housing office, school, hospital or tax inspector can access any individual Social Credit file. Those multi-users can also make limited input."

"I know all that."

"I'm just thinking out loud. The master data is

stored here in London. There are copies at four other regional centres. The base areas are fireproof, flood-proof and guarded by armed anti-terrorist squads. Plus, you might have noticed important computers always live in the sub-ground levels of tower blocks."

"What difference does that make?"

"It means that even if you exploded an airburst nuclear device right over the roof, the hardware and storage would be shielded by twenty stories of collapsing concrete. Instant bunkers – they've got separate hostilities-only entrances and communications lines."

"Good to know that when we're gone, there will still be a machine adding up our parking fines."

"Isn't it reassuring?"

"But you'd already talked me out of that idea. What else is there?"

"Kerry, you're not taking this seriously. Listen, Social Credit is a table-driven system. At the Department, where my mum cleans, they have the database and weighting tables. The satellites hold the processing programmes. So an operator in Manchester, say, can use the system, but not make changes to it except those that come down the line from London. There's a routine for updating the tables in every copy. After the budget, for instance, they will utilise the mass update system to change everybody's Social Credit rating."

"How come you know all this?"

"The outline specification from when they invited tenders for the new system isn't classified. And I've been reading up on it."

"I suppose you're only bluffing, but you make it sound as though you are more familiar with the design philosophy of this bloody system than its creator."

"There isn't one. Creator, that is. Whole teams of programmers worked on it. Like if lord god almighty had been a committee, we might have got Genesis over with in about ten years instead of a week and no-one would know how it was done."

"Don't tell me no-one knows how the Social Credit system works?"

"Almost no-one. There's too much of it to know off by heart, with the additions and changes that have been written in. Not that it matters – they don't really need to know exactly how it got to be what it is. It still runs."

"What do you mean, almost no-one?"

"There is one guy. He's a bit of an oddball. I'll tell you about him later."

"I feel like I'm in a third level infotec lesson. Tell me the rest of it then."

Al grinned. "You sure you want to hear it?"

"Sure I'm sure. Get on with it."

"Some fixes are circulated to the whole network every twelve hours. So twice a day, everything reflects the main logic. Anything that goes into the system at the main centre will be sent out to the other centres which automatically incorporate it. So all four back-ups contain any inserts that the system accepts, including anything I put in, or you, or the office cat."

"If you can get to the database or the weighting tables?"

"Yes."

"Which you haven't done yet, have you?"

"No, I've only been into individuals' files."

"Go on then."

"This system has been running about ten years. The logic is easier to corrupt. The first couple of years, they would have looked real close for errors. But it has been performing like it's meant to for so long, the checks have become a routine chore. Very low grade. And nobody is standing over the drone who does the checks anymore, making sure they are run. So chances are, they don't get done." Al took a cigarette and offered one to Kerry.

"There are two things we could do."

"We?" Kerry interrupted.

"I was kind of hoping I could count you in."

"Don't take it for granted."

"Oh, Kerry. . ."

"What two things could you do?"

"We could insert a programme into the system to update key fields on all records. We could tell it to replace any weighting less than five with a number greater than five. It reads my file, sees my Social Credit rating is 2.2, or whatever, changes it to 8.8 and vice versa. Once it has changed the data item, it writes back to file and goes on to the next one. This system can hit 8,000 records per minute. There are fifty five million people in the UK. So it takes 4.75 days to work that out. Three instructions: read my programme, run my programme, and at the end of the sequence, delete these three lines so no-one knows what's been done."

"I'm sure it's not that simple. You probably make it sound easy because you're missing out all the complicated bits you don't know about."

"I suppose," Al frowned. "You could be right. But sometimes it's better not to try to be too clever. You can imagine difficulties that don't exist."

"That's a good excuse," Kerry smiled, "but I have heard that simple interventions can do the most damage to a sophisticated system."

"There you are then." Al looked relieved.

"I haven't been converted yet."

"These are just ideas, Kerry. They could be changed."

"Go on, tell me about your other schemes."

"OK. The second thing we could do is insert a new weighting table, using the mass update. It doesn't have to be coherent, we could put any old garbage in. The system would be so distorted, it would end up meaningless. Or we could do a simple reversal of the weightings. Maximum points for being a deaf brat in the slums. I think I prefer the garbage option."

"That's got even more simple appeal. What about back-ups? Wouldn't they just retrieve a sound copy of the table?"

"They use forward recovery. All the transactions are backed up to the close of business. Then they start the next day's back-up on separate tapes. So, say they crash this afternoon. They apply the back-up of today's work to the previous back-ups, to recreate the current situation."

"There's a line to conjure with – 'Want to come back to my place and recreate the current situation?'"
"Yes, please."
"You don't count, you're here already. On with the lecture."
"Well, the only trouble is, it takes a lot of capacity. So after the back-up has been stored a week, the tapes are wiped and used to store the new back-up. So, if you make some change to the system whose logic appears to be correct, at the end of seven days, all the back-up tapes are full of the information you created, and there is no record of the original system. That, I reckon, would take some unscrambling."
"Piece of piss."
"Basically, it is."
"Won't they spot it straight away? When dossers start getting rehoused."
"They might do. But more likely it would take some time for the news to get back about what was going on. The system is very centralised, the programmers never have to meet the consumers."
"I still don't know why you need me. Apart from as an admiring audience. You know ten times more about all this than I do."
Al shifted her chair round and stared at Kerry speculatively. "I need to do the business actually in the Department of Social Credit itself."
"Why? I thought you always hacked from home?"
"I can get into individual files from any computer. I simulate the local housing office terminal, I know their pass codes. But to get into the table or main system, I'd have to log in as an authorised user. An out-station wouldn't have that access. Also there's some information I need. About how to get through the last layers of security. I need you to help me find it."
"What information are we going to find lying about in the DSC?" Kerry was sceptical.
"I know it's there," Al was stubborn. "I'll do it alone, if you're afraid, but it's riskier. Two of us would be better."
"Who said anything about being afraid?"

"Aren't you?"

"Yes, maybe I am. I bet you are too."

"Perhaps," Al looked embarrassed. "You'll come though, won't you?"

Kerry thought for a moment. The risk of being caught scared her. She wondered if Al realised how serious it was. She looked at the girl's expectant frown and stubborn jaw. Perhaps she did realise.

"OK," Kerry agreed at last. "You can count me in. Though I must be mad."

"Great." Al beamed at her, relieved. "It won't be for a few days yet. Shall I fill you in on how we get there?"

"Spare no lurid details," Kerry groaned. "I wonder if I'll live to regret this?"

Al, bubbling, outlined her idea. Kerry felt she was being swept along by the force of Al's enthusiasm. She told herself she could always back out, even though she knew it wasn't true.

Al talked on persuasively. Eventually Kerry went back to work on the Credit Transfer file, while Al drifted around looking at things. The computer screen glowed in the increasing darkness and the room filled with cigarette smoke. The grandmother clock in the hall struck eleven.

"Shit, is that clock right?" Al listened to the low chimes.

"It's slow, if anything," Kerry stood up and stretched. "I hadn't realised it was getting so late."

"You've got to play something for me before I go. On your trombone. You said you would."

"At this time of night? I don't think it would go down too well with the neighbours."

"Go on. There's no one else in the house, is there?"

"No, but it is a bit late."

"Just one song. That's all. Why not?"

"People are funny about trombones. Anti-social image they've got."

"I won't go till you play me something. I've never had anyone play a song for me."

Kerry took a look at Al's determined face and gave in. She went upstairs and fetched the instrument.

Back in the living room she shut the window and pulled the heavy curtains, hoping they would muffle the sound. Al sat back expectantly, watching her blow into the mouthpiece to warm it and test the free movement of the slides. Without looking at Al, she did a few warming up harmonics.

"Is that a tune?"

"No, it's just to get me going. This is the tune," she launched into it, playing her favourite thing of the moment. She let the notes out quietly, but the sound still filled the room, curling up to the high ceiling, the low tones being soaked up in the floorboards. She played it through twice and stopped, put the trombone back in its case.

"Well then. There you are."

"What was it? What's it called?"

"Blues for Alice."

"I like that," Al looked tickled. "It was nice."

"I like it too," Kerry relaxed. "I don't usually get to play the melody line. It's a bit of a treat."

"Who does it? I've never heard it before."

"Lots of people play it," Kerry shrugged. "Parker wrote it. Before you were born. Before I was born, come to that."

"Oh," Al nodded understandingly. "Classical."

Kerry strapped up the case and smiled. "Hadn't you better be getting home?"

"Yes," Al hauled herself to her feet. "I guess so. There's a night bus."

"Your mum'll worry you've been out so late," Kerry felt suddenly guilty. "She won't know where you've been. I should have thought. . ."

"Relax. It's none of your business anyway, so don't start getting all responsible."

"But you should have been home hours ago, surely," Kerry paced up and down.

"Mum won't be in from work yet. It'll be fine."

"I don't like you going all the way across town on your own. I'll come with you."

"Don't be stupid. I always go about on my own."

"Oh yeah," Kerry raised her eyebrows. "In the middle of the night? I bet."

"Well it's silly you coming with me," Al sulked. "I don't need you. And then you'd have to come back on your own, so you wouldn't be safe."

"Hold on," Kerry was thinking. "I'm going to pop next door and see if Kath's old banger is on the road. If it is, I'll borrow it and drive you home. OK?"

"OK," Al's assent was grudging. Kerry went out and a few minutes later returned, tossing a key card.

"We're lucky. Not only was she prepared to forgive the late night serenade coming through the wall, she also just got the jalopy back from the garage. You set to go?"

"Yes."

"Let's hit the road. I like driving across town at night."

"So do I," agreed Al, breezily, pulling the front door behind them.

"Oh yes? Do it often, do you?" Kerry led the way to the car. The battery hummed as she started up and edged off the pavement and into the road.

Al grunted and settled back for the ride. Kerry found some music on the all night pirate radio station and hummed as she drove. Out of the corner of her eye she watched Al, sitting with her arms folded and her feet up on the dash, looking like a young tough. She was staring around as the lights of Knightsbridge flitted past the window, enjoying being on the road at night, trying not to show it. Kerry decided to take the long scenic route through the West End.

They hardly spoke on the way to Al's, but it was a comfortable silence. It must be something to do with Al's self-confidence, Kerry told herself.

They reached Al's block and parked carefully under the one street light that was still working in the road. Al jumped out and Kerry followed her into the building.

"Where are you going?" Al demanded.

"I've come all this way, I thought I might as well see you to your door."

"You don't have to."

"I'm an old fashioned girl. Stop arguing." They

trudged up the stairs to the flat. Al opened the front door and half-stepped inside.

"You'd better not leave the car. It'll get pinched."

"No, I'll go now."

"I'd make you a cup of tea," Al looked uncomfortable. Kerry guessed she didn't want her mum coming in and finding strange women around to be explained.

"That's OK, I don't want to be too late back."

"I'm glad I went round yours. After the hospital," Al looked at her feet.

"So am I," Kerry replied.

"You'll think about what I said? Our bit of vandalism? I'd like to do it with you."

"I said you could reckon on me to be there. I won't go back on it." Kerry became aware of drunken voices echoing down the stairwell. "Look, I'd better not hang around. Give me a call, yeah?"

"OK," Al gave her a smile and backed fully into the hall of the flat. "See you."

Kerry waved a hand and turned to go. "Take care." She heard the door snap shut as she reached the stairs.

Donna was waiting at the bus stop when Al got home from school on Monday. She grabbed her daughter by the arm and dragged her up to the flat.

"Just in case you thought you'd slope off until I'd gone to work." Donna's face was grim.

"Mum," Al protested, trying to pull her arm free. The grip was crushing. She allowed herself to be hauled through the front door. "What is it?"

"This," Donna brandished an expensive looking multi-function wrist watch under Al's nose. "Where did you get it?"

'Damn,' Al thought. She had believed that was too small and well hidden for her mum to find. Donna must have been searching her room with fine attention to detail.

"You've been going through my things," she was indignant.

"Alison, I'm waiting for an answer. Where did this come from?"

"You've no right. It's my room. It's private."

Donna slapped her smartly on the side of the leg. "I've every right. I don't like having to poke and pry, and if you weren't such a sneaky, dishonest child, I wouldn't have to. Now tell me where you got this."

"It was given me," Al mumbled sullenly.

"Don't be ridiculous. Who would give you such a thing?"

"A friend."

Donna slapped her again. "Don't make it worse by lying to me. You stole it, didn't you."

Al stared at her, gauging the chances of getting out of it. There were none. She stood squarely facing her mother.

"Well?" Donna demanded again. "Didn't you?"

"So what?" Al stuck out her chin stubbornly. Donna hit her again.

"So, I won't have a child of mine become a thief. How many times have I told you? What we need, I'll get. By working for it. And what we need doesn't include this kind of junk." She dropped the watch on the floor and stepped on it. Al growled. "What do you think would happen to you if I let you grow up believing you could take whatever you wanted?"

"We'd be a lot better off."

"We'd be in prison. Which is where you'll end up, no doubt, but not while I'm responsible for you, you won't."

"Bollocks."

"Don't you swear at me," Donna shouted. Al dodged the flat of her hand. "I don't know what's got into you lately. You never used to be like this."

"You can't make me be who you want me to be," Al shouted back, "I'm not a puppet."

"I can stop you thieving," Donna said, grimly. "I'm getting rid of that wretched computer of yours today. That's what has caused all the trouble."

"Do," Al folded her arms and grinned unpleasantly. "You just do that. I can get another computer. But you'll never get anyone else to do your good deeds for you. Help all your friends out with their Social Credit."

"How dare you?" Donna glared down at her. "Don't you care about all those people you've helped?"

"No."

"You're just saying that."

"How come it's OK to rip off the government, but not to take things I actually want from bloody great rich firms who aren't going to miss it?"

"You'd soon see the difference if you weren't so selfish."

"Tell me about it."

"The Social Credit system is unjust. It's not wrong to help people out when they're being done down by it. No-one suffers."

"The set-up which makes some people stinking rich and says we get nothing is unjust," Al shouted back. "So where's the bloody difference. I don't see it."

"Whether you see it or not, while you live in my house, you'll do as you're told. I'm warning you, I won't stand for you stealing."

"And how long do you think I'm going to stay here?"

Donna smiled. She was back on safe ground.

"You talk so tough, Alison. You're just a child. Where would you go, if you weren't with me?" Al didn't answer. "Nowhere. You know what happens to absconders. You want to be in an institution 'till you're eighteen, just go ahead. She stood aside. "There's the door. No? Well, in that case, go to your room and stay there until I tell you to come out. I forbid you to touch that computer, unless I tell you that you can. If I find you've been disobeying me, I'll keep it locked away, except when you've work to do. I should have done this months ago."

Al stamped sourly to her bedroom, kicking the door aside.

"You'll thank me for this, one day," Donna shouted after her. She desperately wanted it to be true, but she felt she could have handled the scene better. Alison had never been biddable, but surely, Donna felt, she herself used to have more patience with the child's rebelliousness. If only she wasn't so tired all the time. It made her short tempered. She had tried to protect her daughter from the world in which they lived, but it seemed she had failed.

No longer feeling the certainty with which she had dealt with Alison, she hoped her slaps had not been as hard as she had intended at the time.

* * *

On Tuesday afternoon Kerry found Al huddled on the doorstep when she got back from the hospital. The girl had drawn her knees up to her chest with her chin rested on them. Kerry, who was tired and hurrying, didn't notice her until she tripped over her.

"Mind what you're doing."

"Al!" Kerry recovered her balance. "Why are you here?"

"I wanted to see you." Al stood up.

"I suppose you've had a row with your mum?"

"So what's new?" Al shrugged. "Aren't you going to invite me in?"

"Oh alright," Kerry said ungraciously, opening the door. "Did you go to school today?"

"What do you care?"

"I have this horrible feeling I'm going to get blamed for leading you astray."

"I don't need leading. Anyway, they won't know I bunked off."

"Why not?"

"I fixed the register machine."

"Oh god, why couldn't you be an ordinary delinquent?"

Al grinned. "I'll have a coffee thanks." She settled herself comfortably in the living room.

Kerry fussed around, disturbed by the visit, not wanting to ask herself why. Al watched, amused, saying nothing. Eventually, when Kerry had finished all the tasks she had found to do, she sat down opposite Al and frowned at her suspiciously.

"I suppose you want something?"

"It's a social call," Al sounded hurt. "Why are you so touchy?"

"I don't believe you trekked all the way over here to pass the time of day. Tell me the worst. What are you after?"

Al put her feet on the small table between them. "Well, I happen to want a new identity, but that's not why I came to see you."

"Aha!"

"Aha, nothing. I could do it myself. I don't need your help. I thought you might be interested."

"I don't know why, but I find your self-sufficiency frightening. Do you need anyone's help for anything?"

"Maybe."

"But not for this."

"No. Though I was kind of hoping I could use your computer."

"Feel free. I suppose one day you'll turn up with a scheme for world domination and need to borrow our hardware for a few minutes to get it running."

"I'll let you know."

"Thanks a bunch. What do you want a new identity for, anyway?"

"So's I can leave home without being put on the missing children's register."

"Things that bad?"

"Worse. I can't stick it. Me and her might as well be on different planets."

"Where would you go?"

"Anywhere. I could go abroad."

"Not a chance. You'd never get an exit visa."

"Why not?"

"Because no matter what it said on your ID, there is no way anyone would believe you were over eighteen. And you know minors aren't permitted to travel alone long-distance."

"Don't I look eighteen?"

"No."

"Oh," Al was crestfallen. Kerry decided to take advantage of the moment.

"And if you cooked up an ID for yourself that said you were eighteen, it would be spotted for a fake straight away."

"Well," Al sighed. "I'll have to be sixteen then. It's not as good, but it'll do."

"Al, you're impossible," Kerry was exasperated. "Why do you want to risk being chased by the police for the next four years because you've had a row with your mum? If you're under-age and away from home without permission, you'd be virtually on the run."

"That's the whole point of getting another identity. And anyway, it's not just 'a row'. She's impossible. She wants me to be someone I'm not."

"Maybe you'll become that person."

"I am who I am," Al stormed. "I'm not just a phase I'm going through."

"All I'm trying to suggest," Kerry picked her words, "is maybe you shouldn't be in such a hurry to commit yourself to a life of crime."

"You're a fine one to talk. Anyway, I already am."

"But at the moment, you've got the choice. You could stop anytime, if it got dangerous or frightening. If you left home, there wouldn't be that choice. You'd have to be breaking rules all the time in order to live."

"I don't scare easy."

"I know. That's what frightens me."

"You can be frightened for both of us then."

"Believe me, I am."

"I don't know why you're being so dull," Al sounded impatient. "Maybe I'd better go, before you decide it's your duty to turn me over to the child protection."

"How dare you?" Kerry was furious.

"Well, you might," Al stared truculently.

"Fuck off. I won't stand for being called a traitor. Especially not by friends."

"Are we friends?"

"Don't push it."

"Because if we are, maybe you should stop trying to tell me what I ought to do, and start giving me a bit of help with what I want to do."

"Jesus, you're the bloody limit. First you insult me, then you expect me to apologise."

"I'm sorry I hurt your feelings."

"Suggesting that I'd shop you to the filth goes a bit beyond hurt feelings."

"Well, I'm sorry."

"Are you?" Kerry looked at her. "Buggered if I can tell. You're a cold fish."

"Anyway," Al got back to the point, "it's no good trying to put me off. I'm not stopping at home much longer."

"Why do you need to use my computer?"

"You lot, when you want a false ID, you find someone who died young and take over theirs, yeah?"

"Did I tell you that?"

"Yes."

"I shouldn't have done."

"Anyway, there's always the chance that the births and deaths are going to catch up with each other."

"It does happen."

"So, instead of looking for a real person who died, I'm going to hack my way into the Registry of Births computer and invent an identity for myself."

"The electronic virgin birth."

"What do you reckon?"

"Sounds risky to me."

"Why?"

"Because it's an unfamiliar system. Who knows what safeguards they've got?"

"We'll see. But even if it's not the same actual system as the Social Credit use, there's some things about getting in and out of those setups that don't change."

"Yeah, the principles may be the same, but it's the details that catch you out."

"Anyway, I want to try."

"I can see that."

"If I don't do it here, I'll find somewhere else."

"I'm sure. What's wrong with your own kit anyway?"

"Mum's taken it away."

"Doesn't she approve of your free enterprise?"

"If only she knew the half of it."

"Lucky for her she doesn't." Kerry thought for a moment. "Alright, go ahead. But for christ's sake, if Marlene or Ruth come in, don't tell them what you're doing."

"Why not?"

"I don't think they'd approve."

"You don't approve."

"Not really."

"So what's the difference?"

"I don't approve, but I'm going to let you do it. If they found out, they'd give me a hard time for not having stopped you. Marlene because she wouldn't like to think of you taking the risk and Ruth because she enjoys giving me a hard time."

"I'll be as quick as I can." Al went over to the

computer and settled comfortably down to work. Kerry found she couldn't stand to watch, and went upstairs to change out of her work clothes.

Her room was an attic, with a music stand in the corner under the skylight. Piles of sheet music lay on the floor. One wall was covered in photographs, taken last summer, of Kerry being happy with a woman who had since left her.

She felt calmer after a bath. In the corridor, as she dripped her way back to her room, she met Ruth, bristling with suspicion.

"There's a young woman downstairs," Ruth began.

"That's Al."

"Playing with the computer."

"I told her she could."

"She says," Ruth's voice was heavy with disbelief, "that she's filling in an application for the civil service school."

"Ah, hmm, yes," Kerry edged round the other woman, clutching her towel. Marlene bounded up the stairs.

"Hiya," she smiled at them both. "Hey, Kerry, who's the girl in the living room?"

"Al. She's a friend of mine."

"Oh yes?" Marlene and Ruth looked at each other with raised eyebrows. Kerry fled into her room. She was still drying herself when someone knocked. Expecting one of her co-residents, primed with curiosity, she called out 'Come in'.

Al kicked the door shut behind her and stood staring. Kerry's skin was flushed pink from the hot water, her small, smooth body gleamed with the afternoon sun behind her. Al smiled. This was as she had imagined. Kerry read the approval in her look, and also the shyness. Quickly, she pulled on her clothes, dragging a shirt roughly over her head.

"Bit cold in here," she explained, awkwardly. Al said nothing. She wondered how these things happened. Kerry seemed shaken. She could be nervous. She could be embarrassed. It was possible she felt the same as Al, but there was no way of telling. If she did, surely she wouldn't be hunting for her socks?

"I gather you met the others?" Kerry chatted on, a bit too fast.

"Yes." Al stuck her hands in her pockets and leaned against the wall. "The snappy one wanted to know what I was doing."

"That would be Ruth. I'm surprised she didn't mistake you for a police spy. Lucky you're not old enough."

"Isn't it just?"

There was an uncomfortable pause. Kerry finished dressing. She avoided looking at Al as much as possible.

"How did it go?" she asked, to fill the silence.

"What?"

"Your new ID. Did you get into the registry?"

"Oh, that. Yes. I got in."

"Was it OK?"

"I'll find out when I go for a copy of the birth certificate."

"Be careful, hey?"

"Sure."

"Look, Al, maybe it's time you were getting home."

"Is it?"

"You weren't planning on leaving your mum's without a new ID?"

"Maybe not."

"Anyway, I've got a house meeting with Ruth and Marlene. They're moving out tomorrow and we have to sort out about bills and things. Actually, it should have started already. So I'll have to go to that."

"Uh huh."

"OK?"

"Don't worry, I can take a hint." Al gave Kerry a hard, unreadable stare, peeled herself off the wall and ran quickly downstairs. Kerry heard the front door slam and swore crossly to herself.

The house meeting was the same as always, underlying tensions not mentioned, surface irritations discussed at great and reasonable length. They all sounded pleasant and considerate. Kerry wondered if it wouldn't be better if she and Ruth threw plates at each other and shouted, but it wasn't done. When they had finished pretending to be civilised adults, Ruth dragged Marlene off for a post-mortem. Kerry stretched herself out on the living room sofa, propped her feet on the entertainment centre and thought about suppressed violence.

The doorbell rang, surprising Kerry. It was late, and they weren't expecting visitors that she knew of. Maybe she shouldn't go and see, in case it was the police. But they would only kick it down, and if she didn't go, there was a chance she would miss someone interesting.

Al stood outside waiting for an answer to her ring. She managed to look more self-assured than she felt. The door was opened a crack and Kerry's nose appeared round it, cautiously followed by the rest of her face. Al struck a tough stance, fists on her hips.

"Did you get through with your meeting?"

"Al!" Kerry flung the door wide and stared. "I thought you went home."

"Why? I never said I was going to. Mind if I come in?" She shouldered her way past Kerry and marched down the hall.

"Look, hang on a bit Al," Kerry protested, following her. "You really have to go home. We could both get into trouble. Your mum might report you."

"She thinks I'm at my cousin's. Anyway, she's gone out to work by now, so who's to know?"

"It sounds almost as though you set this up. Not that I believe you. We'll probably have a squad of child-catchers round here in nothing flat."

"No-one knows I'm here," Al soothed.

"What do you want?" Kerry eyed her suspiciously.

"Can I stay the night?"

"And if I say no?"

Al shrugged. "I'll shove off if you like. I'm not bothered. But I'm not going home. Not tonight."

"So I'll be responsible if you end up roaming the streets? Thanks a bunch."

"Responsible nothing. I'm not looking for another mother. It's no business of yours where I am if I'm not here."

"Oh yeah?" Kerry cast a jaundiced eye over her options. "If I let you stay, will you go home tomorrow? I mean, you're not moving in or anything."

"Sure. I'm not ready to move out from there yet. I need a bit of time off, that's all."

"I can't really refuse, can I?" Kerry grumbled. "You'd better sleep on my floor. I don't want to have to explain you to the others."

"Am I such a problem?"

"Yes," Kerry looked at her uncomfortably. "You are. Come on upstairs and I'll find you a sleeping bag."

She led the way to her room and fussed around finding bedding. "The bathroom is down the corridor," she explained. "If you want to clean your teeth, the stuff on the second shelf is mine. I'm going to take my lenses out, then it's all yours."

When she got back, Al was sitting in a pile of folded quilts, smoking. Kerry unrolled her own bed and beat the pillows into shape. She found herself avoiding looking at her guest.

"If you want to go out," Al said, calmly, "don't feel you've got to stop in on my account."

"I wasn't going anywhere."

"I thought you might be going to one of your bars."

"Lucky for you I didn't. I can't see the others giving you house room for the night."

"What do you do? When you go to a bar?"

"Drink. Meet friends. What do you think?"

"Pick up women?"

"Jesus, Al, where did you get that idea from?"

"Must be something you said. Isn't that what you do though?"

"You make me sound like a human forklift. Maybe I do cruise around a bit, now and again, but it's nothing to write home about."

"No?"

"No," Kerry said firmly.

"Guess I'll go and have a wash," Al stood up. Kerry waited until she was out of the room, then turned off the light and got herself undressed and into bed. She lay in the twilight halogen glow coming from the street through the unshaded skylight. Al returned, neatly undressed and sat down on the edge of Kerry's futon.

"Kerry?"

"Uh huh?"

"Can we talk?" Her voice was gruff and carefully casual.

"Don't you think it should wait? It's late, and I've got to be up for work in the morning."

"Are you sleepy?"

"No," Kerry admitted.

Al stretched out her hand tentatively, looking at it as though it belonged to something else. It came to rest on Kerry's shoulder. Al's fingers, cold and not steady, curled round and stroked the back of Kerry's neck.

Kerry felt the veins in her groin pulse with a sudden rush of blood. She grabbed Al's wrist and struggled to sit up. Al, taking advantage of the movement, leaned forward and kissed her.

"What are you doing?"

"What do you think?"

"This is absurd, Al. It's just not on."

"I want to sleep with you."

"You can't." Finding she still had hold of the girl's wrist, she let it go. "It's out of the question."

"Why?"

"Isn't it obvious? You're too young."

"How old were you when you first knew you wanted to do it with a woman?" Kerry didn't answer. "Same age as me, huh?"

"OK, so you're old enough to know what you want," Kerry pulled the quilt around her and tried to keep her eyes off Al's round breasts and wide shoulders. Eye contact wasn't much better. "Go and find someone your own age to try it all out on." She sounded crueller than she had meant, but she didn't trust herself.

"What's age got to do with it? I want you, why should I go looking for someone I don't care about, just because she was born the same year as I was?"

"I didn't mean that."

"It's what it sounded like. Doesn't matter who you

pick up, so long as she's a suitable age. Is that what you did?"

"No, look Al, I didn't mean it the way it sounded. I'm really pleased for you. I'm flattered you told me. But I don't think we would be good for each other."

"That's bullshit. You're just frightened."

"Oh yeah?" Kerry was riled. "What am I frightened of? Apart from getting locked up, of course, which I would if I had anything to do with you. Or being beaten up by your mum?"

"I don't know what you're scared of. What your friends would think. All that shit you heard about kids. You think you'd be in charge and I'd be helpless. That's crap and you know it."

"Not much danger of anyone feeling in charge when you're around," Kerry tried to laugh, but croaked on it. "Face it, Al, I'm the first lesbian you've met. It's not surprising you feel like this."

"Don't patronise me. You're not the first I've met, and I didn't fall for you just because you were there."

"Look, Al, I don't think it would work. Can't you accept that? I'm not interested in having an affair with you."

"If you can't handle being an older woman. . ."

"At nineteen? I should bloody well say not."

". . . then that's your problem," Al continued. She started to run a finger slowly up Kerry's side, counting the ribs. "But don't try and tell me that you're not interested."

"It's not possible. I told you."

"But you want to, don't you?" she brushed her fingers lightly across Kerry's nipple.

"Yes, dammit, I want to but I can't. Leave me alone."

"Why can't you?" Al took her hand away with an effort.

"It feels wrong."

"Scruples."

"Maybe. Even having said I want to sleep with you feels wrong. I hadn't even thought it to myself until you started in with all this."

"You were lying to yourself then."

"Not telling the whole truth maybe."

"Why?"

"It's frightening. You've got to understand. You see something you want and can't see any reason why we shouldn't do it. It isn't that simple for me. It feels wicked."

"You'll get over it."

"Oh god," Kerry collapsed onto her pillows. "Does this mean you're planning to pursue me until I give in?"

"No," Al lay down carefully beside her, putting an arm around her. "I just live in hope."

"Don't think that because you're in bed with me means I've agreed."

"I don't," Al murmured, stroking the flat of her palm over Kerry's stomach, feeling the muscles bunch under her touch.

"You needn't get comfortable," Kerry felt the breath catching in her throat. "You're not staying."

"No?"

"We wouldn't get a very restful night."

"Me quivering with lust and you with moral panic?"

"Shit, Al, I wish I didn't like you so much."

"Why?"

"It would make it easier."

"I'll go." Al swung her legs across Kerry's body and rolled out of bed. She pulled on her jeans and started looking for her shoes.

"Where are you going?"

"I don't want to give you a hard time."

"It's the middle of the night."

"I can take care of myself."

"I know you can."

"Are you asking me to stay?"

"Please stay."

"Is that because you're worried about me, or because you want my body?" Al finished dressing and knelt by the bed, peering into Kerry's face.

"You could always sleep in the living room."

"No thanks. Don't worry, I've got money, I'll take a taxi."

"Why are you so bloody independent?"

"Who knows? Can I kiss you?" Without waiting for an answer, she kissed Kerry, more accurately than the first time. "I'll see you again?"

"Yes," Kerry sighed. "With your persistence, I don't doubt it." Al squeezed her hand and stood up. Kerry saw her smile, then, closing the door quietly behind her, she left.

"What do you think?" Ruth asked Marlene, looking around their new home. "White isn't too clinical, is it?"

"No. Especially not in this heat." Ruth put down her paintbrush and wiped the sweat out of her eyes. "It feels strange to be decorating a place that isn't actually falling down. I've got used to papering over cracks."

"It's small, isn't it?" Ruth paced around anxiously.

"But so respectable."

"I don't know how we're going to share out the shelves."

"Relax." Marlene pulled Ruth towards her and kissed the frown off her paint-spattered brow. "I can always put up more shelves. It's the perfect home for a one-income-no-kids couple."

"You're worrying about the rent, aren't you? I told you I don't mind paying more than half. I can afford it."

"I'm not going to be a kept woman forever, though. I'll have to pick up a bit of work."

"It's quite cheap, for what it is," Ruth tried to reassure herself.

"Of course it is. They couldn't sell it."

"I suppose no one would buy into a basement, these days."

"What are we going to do when the Thames Barrier bursts?"

"Head for the hills."

"You have to laugh," Marlene said, sitting on the floor. "If I get a job, I'm going to buy a settee."

"A brand new one?"

"Isn't it wicked? I'll get recycled cushions, if that makes you feel any better."

"I suppose I do feel a bit guilty about all this. . ."

"No!" interrupted Marlene, with feigned incredulity.

". . . partly because I'm so glad not to be living with Kerry anymore."

"I'm sure the relief is mutual."

"Do you think so? I worry about her rattling about in that great barn all alone."

"I worry about her rattling about not alone," sniffed Marlene.

"What do you mean?"

"That girl, whatsername, Al."

"You don't think?" Ruth's jaw dropped.

"Al does though, if I'm not mistaken. Kerry doesn't know what's hit her."

"I did hear someone turn up very late, that last night we were there."

"So did I."

"But," said Ruth, looking worried. "Think of the trouble she'd get in, if she was caught. I'm not sure I approve anyway. There's such an age difference."

"Kerry's just a kid herself."

"You would never have dared say that when she was living with us."

"No, but it's true. She's closer in age to Al than she is to either of us," Marlene pointed out.

"But she's always gone for older women," objected Ruth.

"Perhaps that's because she's always been around older women. Anyway, now I reckon she's being gone after herself."

"Well, I'm shocked. Does that make me an old fogey?"

"It does indeed, my love. But that kind of goes with the territory of being a householder."

"I don't want to sink into apolitical self-indulgence."

Marlene snorted. "Chance would be fine thing. I'm sure this absorption in matters domestic is only temporary."

"It does feel a bit like being on holiday," admitted Ruth. "I've been thinking about the Credit Transfer group." Marlene groaned, but Ruth ignored her. "We will be able to start up again, but this time, I want to be a bit more professional about it."

"You mean, make them pay? Now I'm shocked."

"No, what I had in mind was a better organised group. Smaller, more security conscious. Perhaps with Kath and a couple of the less flighty ones. That great sprawling collective was hopeless for security."

"Good at meetings though. What about Kerry?"

"I don't think her heart is really in it, do you?"

"Perhaps she has other preoccupations."

"Anyway, I want a structure that allows no direct contact between any of us and the groups we help. Kerry would always be getting emotionally involved with this organisation or that, and wanting to do them favours."

"A structure! My word, you have been reviewing your priorities."

"It's only a matter of luck that we're not all in gaol at the moment."

"And skill," protested Marlene.

"But mostly luck. And much good we could have done from prison. I don't want to take unnecessary risks anymore."

"And besides, it's so much more comfortable here?" suggested Marlene.

"With that," said Ruth, snuggling against her lover, "I can't argue."

* * *

Kerry spent the rest of the week trying to convince herself that she wasn't unnerved by Al's advances. She went about in a state of turmoil. Returning to the empty silence of her home on Thursday, she checked her mailbox, and found a message flagged for her. Punching it up, she saw, with a sinking heart, that the sender was Al.

"Don't Panic," the first line scrolled rapidly up the screen, "this=business. Ready to go tomorrow night. Call me for time and entry port. No tricks or games."

Kerry wondered whether this was the start of the campaign of seduction, despite the reassurance, but decided that lack of directness was not Al's problem. Kerry was overwhelmed by confusion. She wanted to go to sleep for a week and wake up when all difficult things had gone away. She looked with irritation at the message. Al might be a criminal, but she wasn't dishonest. If she said it was business, then that's what it was.

Kerry considered the wisdom of getting involved in Al's brand of electronic terrorism. It was rash, it was risky. The Credit Transfer group wouldn't approve. Plus she should be avoiding Al until any temptation to take up her ridiculous proposition was past. Why was she even considering jeopardizing her personal comfort like this? Having determined that the sensible thing would be to ignore the message, she poured herself a stiff Rumanian Tequila and called up Al to count herself in.

* * *

The security guard at the Department of Social Credit watched the night-cleaners come in. Half the faces he didn't recognise, the turn-over was so high. He was a friendly type, who missed the old days, before jobs like his and the cleaners' had been privatised. Then you could get to know people, seeing the same ones day in, day out for years.

He smiled at Donna as she struggled through the small side door on its heavy spring.

"Evening, Mrs Treece."

"Evening, Shaun."

"Got the kid with you, I see," he winked at Al. It was against the rules, but a few of the cleaners brought their children in with them. He was a family man himself, and didn't like to think of kids being left alone while their mothers were out at work.

"That's right. Didn't like to leave her by herself." She nodded to him and passed by, with Al in tow, smiling her best little girl smile.

Kerry tugged at the headscarf knotted under her chin, took a deep breath and walked into the building. She let her overcoat hang open to show the uniform of the company who had the cleaning contract. She hitched the handles of her shopping bag further up her arm and walked to the security desk. She tried to keep in mind the three most boring things in the world, so that her face would stay blank and her voice not shake.

"Hullo," she said. The security man looked up. "I'm a stand-in. They sent me over to sub for one of the women who's off sick."

"Which one?"

"Don't know, do I? They didn't tell me who it was. Just said to get over here if I wanted the work and report to the supervisor."

"I wish they'd tell me," he grumbled, "then I could give you her pass and save a lot of bother. I'll have to make you out one now."

"I've got my compay ID," Kerry pulled back her coat to show the oblong badge pinned onto her overall. "Won't that do?"

"Give us it here," he commanded. She unclipped the badge and handed it over. He peered at it. "I'll tell you what I'll do," he said ponderously, thinking hard. "You wear that for tonight, and I'll sign it, in case anyone asks." He took out a marker and wrote laboriously on the back of the plastic oblong. "And you get your firm to send a chit to our security people tomorrow so we can have a pass ready for you when you come in to work tomorrow night."

"Right," Kerry pinned the badge back onto her chest.

"I shouldn't really let you in without a pass," he obviously expected to be thanked.

"Ta," Kerry smiled sweetly. "I can't be doing with all this red tape, myself."

"Rules is rules," he said sternly, then winked. "But you know what they say about rules?"

"Made to be broken?" Kerry was anxious to be off.

"Stretched a little, shall we say. Yes, you have to be a bit elastic in my job. You know, this whole place would grind to a halt if we stuck to the letter of the rules."

"Always the way, isn't it?" Kerry started to walk past. "I must be getting off, or the supervisor'll be thinking I didn't show up."

"Down that corridor, first left you want," he pointed the direction. "She'll be in the rest room doing the assignments."

"Ta," she set off briskly.

"Cheerio, Mrs Gentry," he called after her, but in the time it took Kerry to remember her borrowed name, she was at the corner of the passageway and turning out of his sight.

Al was waiting in the sub-basement. She was carrying a portable garbage compressor, but no-one took any notice of her. Most of the women who brought their kids in with them gave them some work to do. There was nothing else to keep them out of trouble and under the cleaner's eye. She heard footsteps coming down the stairs fast, and Kerry appeared, looking pale. She smiled quickly, but avoided looking Al in the eye. Her awkwardness was overcome by Al's business-like tension.

"Come over here," Al said quietly, "you've got to take your coat off." She led the way to a cupboard and showed Kerry where to put her outdoor things and basket. Donna was away up the corridor with the waxing machine, there was nobody else about.

"How did it go?"

"Oh," Kerry straightened her overall and took the solvent-dispensing squeegie which was offered. She stuffed her pockets with dusters and a can of anti-static spray. "Pretty much like you said it would be."

"He's a soppy git," Al said, with satisfaction. "You got the uniform with no trouble?"

"One of the women I know moonlighted with the company for a while. Lucky it's the same overall wherever you're working."

Al read the badge Kerry wore. "L. Gentry. What's the L for?"

"Lydia."

"Never!"

"Yes, well, I'm not sure what Kath was thinking of when she invented this identity, but it wasn't one of her restrained periods."

"Hmm," Al grunted, "we'd better get going."

"OK," Kerry looked apprehensive. "You're sure you know where we're headed?"

"Of course," Al set off. "Don't forget your squeegie, Lydia."

They walked quietly along, making a couple of left turns, working their way into the centre of the building. Al stopped in front of an office door. All around them the basement hummed with a low continuous noise. Kerry knew they were very close to the main computer equipment. She leant on the handle of the solvent dispenser and looked around while Al prised open the door lock with a thin flexible blade. There was a click behind her and she turned to see Al slipping into the unlit office. She followed and they locked the door behind them.

"The night operator's running programmes two doors along," Al said quietly as they stood in the dark, "so we can't make too much noise. She goes off for a break at twelve thirty."

"Where's the other one?" Kerry was busy stuffing dusters around the door to block off any gaps.

"He got appendicitis two days ago. The staff won't cover for long absences and the department has overrun its budget, so they can't take on a temp."

"How do you know?"

"Broke into the supervisors' electronic mailbox," Al answered shortly. "You done?"

"Yes." Kerry stood up. "There's no light going to show under that. And it's pretty bright out there anyway."

"OK," Al turned on a desk lamp, pulling the shade down close to the surface of the table so only a small pool of light was cast. She got down on her hands and knees and felt under the bottom drawer of the desk.

"What are you doing?"

"Unlocking his filing drawer." Al pushed up the bar that connected all three drawers on the right hand side of the desk and eased out the deep drawer at the bottom. The metal runners rumbled quietly. Inside, the drawer was crammed with envelopes and folders full of continuation paper. Al divided the stack roughly in half and gave one bundle to Kerry. They sat down on either side of the desk.

"What are we looking for?" Kerry asked.

"This guy is a real dinosaur, right?" Al said, sorting files quickly into a neat pile at her left elbow. "He still uses hard copy to debug and develop before he puts a new programme into the system. He's quite old."

"That explains it."

"Also he's got RSS."

"Radiant Screen Syndrome?"

"Yeah, his brain goes on the blink if he sits in front of any normal frequency emissions for more than an hour. Gets migraines."

"You know a lot about this man."

"Shit, Kerry," Al looked scathing. "You think this is the first time I've been in here? It's taken weeks to read through all the gumph. It's a mess. But this drawer's the only one I haven't been through yet. It's got to be in here."

"Why?"

"He's a senior programmer. Been here since the year dot and quill pens. One of the team who got the system up and running. Bit of an eccentric. He sits and scribbles on his hard copy and leaves the gofers to do the keying-in and syntax debugging. He only deals with the key system programmes. I know what we're looking for is in this stack, because he writes everything down. Hard to believe, but true. And I looked everywhere else already."

"But what's the point of security if you're going to leave the workings of the system lying in your desk drawer?"

"Don't ask me. But I bet hardly anyone knows he keeps all this hard copy. I mean, they're all geared to computer security, they don't expect people to write things down. I only found it by accident when I was snooping around."

"OK," Kerry took out the first scribbled programme and started reading it. "I suppose we're looking for the mass-update routine, yeah? So we can change the rating assumptions and input your programme to garbagize the weightings table."

"Think you'd recognise it?"

"Yes, should do. What about the log-on sequence for an authorised user."

"I got that already."

They worked their way in silence through the papers. Kerry could hear her heart pounding. Her mouth was dry. Al scanned quickly down the lines, making little grunting sounds. Twenty minutes passed like a week. After an hour, Kerry was convinced they were on a wild goose chase. When she finally found the mass-update routine, she had to read it twice to make sure. The figures jumped about in the lamplight.

"Got it," she whispered. Al snatched the page out of her hand and read it, nodding to herself. "What now?"

"What's the time?"

"Half past," Kerry looked at her watch, the numbers glowing red. "There's no one on the computer just now?"

"No. We've got fifteen minutes. Maybe a bit less."

"Shall we do the deed?"

"I reckon." Al walked over to the terminal on the other side of the office. It hadn't been switched off for the night. She sat down in front of the screen and put the programmer's notes beside her.

"Can you log on from this terminal?"

"Yes," Al muttered. "Could you put a bit of light on this for me?" she asked Kerry. The desk lamp was moved and Al began. Kerry stood at her shoulder and watched. She heard footsteps outside the door and went rigid with fear, but whoever it was carried on past. Al was oblivious.

After five minutes of inactivity, Kerry was getting so nervous she could hear the sweat trickling down her scalp. She started pacing up and down the office, three steps each way, careful not to walk into the furniture. Time crawled past.

"That's it," Al said suddenly. Kerry jumped.

"What?"

"That's it. All done. The computer is now busily engaged on chewing up its own insides. Couldn't stop it if I wanted to."

"Let's get out of here then."

"Aren't you pleased?" Al couldn't keep a grin from splitting her face.

"Yes, I'm pleased," Kerry snapped. "I'm also scared shitless that we're going to get caught."

"It's waiting around that's got to you," Al looked contrite. "I should have let you do some of it. Sorry."

"Don't apologize" Kerry relented, gave Al a small buffet on the shoulder. "You hog all the fun, why not? It was your idea. But I do think we should be going."

"You're right," Al stood up and collected the papers and files they had used. Quickly bundling them together, she shovelled them back into the desk drawer and locked it with her pocket knife. She turned off the lamp, and Kerry collected all the dusters from around the door. Cautiously they looked out into the corridor. There was no-one in sight. Kerry slid out of the office, with Al following, pulling the door shut and relocking it. Trying not to hurry, they walked out of the restricted area. Kerry's heart lurched each time they passed an office or turned a corner, expecting every moment shouts and running footsteps in pursuit. Al sauntered along looking wide-eyed about her, but with her fists clenched in tension.

No security guards lumbered after them, no alarms sounded. They were not stopped. Nothing happened and they arrived back at the broom cupboard.

"You'll have to hang around until the end of the shift," Al said, her voice a little tight and unnatural. She coughed to clear her throat and tried again. "Push an ioniser around or something, and then just leave with all the others."

"Sure thing," Kerry pulled out a packet of cigarettes. "You want one?"

Al looked longingly at the offered tobacco. "Better not, my mum's around here somewhere and she'd go spare."

Kerry laughed. She propped herself weakly against the wall and held her sides. She shook with silent chuckles. Her hysteria threshold felt very low. Al eyed her with suspicion.

"What's cracking you up?"

"You are. You've just maybe destroyed the entire Social Credit system, practically single handed, and what you're really worried about is your mum catching you smoking."

"Keep your voice down, will you?" Al shushed.

"Sorry." Kerry pulled herself together. "But it's been a bit of a funny night."

"I know," Al was fidgeting to be off.

"How do you feel?"

"Not bad," she shrugged, "bit wobbly inside maybe."

"Me too."

"Nothing we can do now. Just wait. If they haven't picked up on it in a week, we've done it. Otherwise. . ." she pulled a face.

"It's going to be hard, waiting."

"Yeah."

"We'd better not see each other till then," Kerry suggested.

"Oh yes?" Al raised her eyebrows sardonically. "Security, is it?"

"Something like that," Kerry was embarrassed.

"You haven't changed your mind about the other thing?"

"I suppose I've been trying not to think about it."

"Liar."

"Perhaps."

"You're scared, aren't you?"

"Yes."

"We make a good team," Al stared at her seriously. "I'll see you in seven days time."

"Take care of yourself, Al," Kerry said inadequately.

"You're the one who should take care." Al's face

smoothed out into a smile. "Who's going to suspect me of anything? I'm just a kid."

"Likewise me," Kerry smiled back. "I'm just a cleaning woman."

"Well then," Al got within an inch of giving Kerry a hug, then thought better of it and stuck her hands in her pockets. "See you around."

"Yes. See you."

Al walked off, down the corridor. At the far end she broke into a run. Kerry watched her go, picked up her squeegie to polish off the time before she could leave.

* * *

The night operator came back from her tea break and settled down to run the next batch of programmes that were waiting. While the computer did its business, she knitted a sock. It was no concern of hers who had written the programmes, or what was in them.

Neatly turning a heel, she checked her schedule for the rest of the shift. Another table update. She resented the Chancellor's constant stream of budgets, mini-budgets and financial statements. Tinkering with the economy. More work for the likes of her. But the night operator was a free-market liberal, and took the endless adjustments of the Social Credit system as a personal insult. Disapprovingly, she punched in the run update code, then doubled her yarn and knitted calmly on.

Al struggled with the note she was writing her mum. Five years ago she had often run away from home, and always left a note. Before that, when she was too young to write, she would take her duvet and the biscuit tin, so Donna would realise that she had gone.

Running away in those days had never involved going further than Anji's flat, or the nearest park. If Donna didn't come and find her before she got bored, or finished the biscuits, she would go home and reproach her mum for not caring enough.

It would be easier if she was furious with Donna, as she had been after their last row about stealing. But the rage had worn into sullenness. Donna might be impossible, but she did try. Coming home exhausted yesterday, she had suggested they both go up to Lea Valley for a couple of hours ice skating in the cut-price morning session. They used to skate every week, when Al was younger. It was one of the things that had been dropped as Donna took on extra jobs and sunk deeper into tiredness and irritability.

Al screwed up her face and thought. She had composed this message often enough during the days after one of their frequent arguments. None of those terse, triumphant put-downs, which she had so carefully polished, seemed appropriate to the occasion. To her disgust, she found herself concerned to alleviate Donna's worry, hoping her mum would not be lonely. At the same time as she pictured Donna stamping on her new watch, she saw her leading a younger Al, barely steady on her legs, across a crowded ice-rink, laughing. Her tear ducts prickled and she bent to her task.

She had tried a dozen times to compose something that did not sound babyish, but all her attempts were clumsy. Exasperated, she assembled a few sentences which explained her absence in the least mawkish way. Not knowing how to finish off gave her pause. Eventually she added an extra line, "I love you", signed it "Al" and propped the note against the teapot on the table.

* * *

Kerry checked her watch again. A stream of people trudged across Ravenscourt Park on their way home from work. She balanced her coffee cup on the shaky metal table and shooed away the crowd of pigeons who hung around the tea-rooms.

Al strode across the grass, hands in pockets, a bag slung over her shoulder. She came to a halt in front of Kerry and stared down at the seated woman. Kerry's heart thumped. "I'm getting too old for this," she thought.

"Well?" she croaked.

"We did it." Al rumpled her hair. "Fixed the bastards."

Kerry let out a long sigh of relief. She felt as if she had been holding her breath for a week.

"You sure?"

"Yes." Al pulled up a chair and lit a cigarette. Her eyes gleamed with excitement. "I checked Phyllis Zwemmer's Social Credit rating today. 9.9. It was 1.1 last week. They sequence alphabetically, so that's all done."

"What about the weighting tables?" Kerry glanced over her shoulder to make sure no-one was listening.

"I've seen the night operator's work-schedules for the last seven days. Totally routine. If they'd spotted what we did, those operators would have dropped everything to input a clean version of the original table. But nothing. No flap, no security panic. They didn't notice."

"And now it's too late?"

"You bet," Al grinned. "The tables are full of

garbage. Our garbage is on all the back-ups. They've no record of the assumptions on which they based the calculation of everybody's Social Credit rating. I went and swiped the hard copy from the senior programmer's office last night. Put it in the shredder sack."

"You went back in there? On your own?"

"So?" Al looked nonchalant. "It was straightforward. Only took a couple of minutes."

"It was a risk. What if you'd been caught? It would have jeopardised the whole thing."

"I reckon I'm entitled to take a few risks. Shit, it was my idea to start with."

"I know," Kerry grumbled. "I don't like being left out." She helped herself to one of Al's cigarettes. "You're an offensively self-sufficient type."

"You wouldn't think so if I was the same age as you."

"You don't exactly fill a woman with the warm glow of neededness."

"I didn't know that's what you wanted. Maybe you should get a dog? They're pretty needy."

"I think I'll ignore that," Kerry sniffed. "What happens now?"

"To the Social Credit?"

"Yes."

"Everyone's ratings are cock-eyed. Sooner or later they'll realise the tables are stuffed. They've no way of recalculating what all the ratings should have been because we've removed the information and replaced it with junk. I reckon it's so corrupted it'll be useless. They'll have to start again almost from scratch."

"Better than a 'phone box, eh?" Kerry gloated.

"Maybe it won't take long to set it up again. Perhaps they've got a procedure to cover this." Al kicked a pebble.

"Why so gloomy? Whatever happens we've fouled things up for them in a big way. That's what you wanted."

"Yes, I suppose. I'm quite sorry I won't be around to see it."

"Why?" Kerry looked up sharply. "Where are you going?"

"I'm booked on a night flight to Paris." Al reached inside her jacket for an envelope, which she threw on the table between them. "There's a ticket for you. It's undated, in case you need some time to decide."

"But you can't travel alone. Even if you've got a new ID."

"I've got an escort. Don't you worry. One certified adult to see me through immigration," Al sounded pleased with herself. "She's meeting me here."

A bag-lady stumped down the path towards the tea-room. Kerry, who was avoiding Al's eye, not knowing what to say, watched her. As the woman came closer, Kerry realised that although she walked like a vagrant, her clothes were new; the bags she carried were respectable soft luggage. She turned back to the girl sitting opposite.

"Is this an ultimatum? Either I come with you, or you take off abroad for a life of crime and I never see you again?"

"Would that bother you?"

"Yes," Kerry admitted. "It would."

"Come too then."

"I can't."

"Why not?"

"I don't know."

"Same reason you couldn't decide whether to let me stay the night," Al scowled. "You're afraid."

"You keep saying that," Kerry protested.

"It's true. Lots of things frighten you."

"But none as much as being swept off my feet by a girl like you."

"Think about it." Al stood up. "Hi," she greeted the woman in new clothes. "Glad you made it." They shook hands.

"Haven't been to Paris since I was a girl." The woman heaved herself into a chair. "Fancied the trip. She coming too?"

"She doesn't know yet," Al explained.

"What's keeping you?" the newcomer growled. Kerry shrugged. She noticed how sunburnt and tough the woman's skin was.

"Here's your ID." Al handed over a plastic card. "Travel permit and tickets. You'd better have mine too, since you're supposed to be in charge." The woman pocketed the documents. "I've opened a Banking Society account for you," Al went on in a business-like fashion. "It's credited with five thousand Europounds. You'll get the rest of what we agreed once I'm in France."

"I'm not fussed," the woman muttered. "I managed without an account all these years. Don't suppose I'll have much use for one now."

"There's the card and your PIN number." Al dealt another bit of plastic.

"I don't know," the woman grumbled. "All this bother. As if it wasn't bad enough having to get dressed up like this."

"You look very smart," Kerry offered.

"Stiff," the woman plucked at the sleeve of her new coat. "Uncomfortable. I liked the old things."

"Immigration wouldn't have though," Al suggested. The woman grumbled on quietly, though Kerry thought she wasn't unhappy. She had an air of anticipation. Al went to get her a cup of tea.

"How did you meet Al?"

"We see each other around," the woman said.

"How come you're going abroad with her?"

"You ever try saying no to that girl when she wants you to do something?" Her thick eyebrows crawled up her forehead like question marks. Kerry blushed. Fortunately, an answer was not required. "Anyway, I like to travel. Broadens the mind."

Kerry sat in the warm evening sun while Al smoked and the woman drank her tea noisily. She tried to think of a single good reason for staying in London. None occurred to her. Stubbornly, she avoided looking at Al.

Eventually the girl stood up and hefted her bag onto her shoulder. The woman, still muttering, hauled herself to her feet.

"We'd better be going," Al said. "I've still got a few things to do." She took Kerry's hand. Their palms jumped slightly at the touch. "How about it?"

"I don't know why you think you can run my life like this," Kerry stormed, trying to be angry.

"It's up to you," Al shrugged. Kerry said nothing.

"Au re-bloody-voir," the woman snorted. Al grinned and let go of Kerry's hand. The two of them walked off towards the park gate. Al turned and waved once.

Kerry watched them out of sight. She got up to go. The ticket, in its envelope, lay where Al had thrown it, like a challenge. It might seem simple to Al, but Kerry knew it wasn't that easy. Still undecided, she put the ticket in her pocket and went home.